Original Prints Four

Original Prints Four

New Writing from Scottish Women

Edited by Elizabeth Burns, Sara Evans,
Thelma Good and Barbara Simmons

Polygon

EDINBURGH

First published in 1992 by Polygon
22 George Square, Edinburgh

Copyright © 1992 Polygon

Typeset by Combined Arts, Edinburgh
Printed and bound in Great Britain by
Billing & Sons, Worcester

British Library Cataloguing In Publication Data

Original prints 4: new writing from Scottish women.
823.01089287 [FS]

ISBN 0 7486 6129 8

Set in Monotype Sabon 10.5 on 13.5pt

Contents

Contents

The Drowning of MacKail

Margaret Elphinstone

DOWN ON the beach, she was bored wretched with emotion, and the midges were out. It was time to put a stop to this. Life was traumatic. OK, life was traumatic. The wind had died in the night, and the day had never properly broken. It hung muggily over the water, a pale lifeless sea that could not bestir itself to make one wave. The grass was still sodden; the dew had never been cleared up after a heavy night. It went on being day because it was not yet time for dusk. The hills had not emerged, however. They remained shrouded; nothing worth rising from the dead for. Only the midges had risen, in their millions. Midges were nothing, with a wound like a dagger's thrust under her ribs. If there were real blood, the insects would have a field day. She imagined them gathering, the gaping red hole turning black as they gorged themselves. But the wound was not real, except insofar as she could feel it.

She had been feeling it now for two weeks, ever since the news broke. So you thought you had a lover. Twist of the knife. She could see his face mirrored in the sea. Not a ripple. Time to put a stop to all this. Get thee behind me. He wouldn't budge. Given the choice, he would come latching on again, all gaping mouth and neediness. Suck, suck. The faintest ripple on the rocks echoed the thought. I'll have to get rid of him myself.

No sooner thought than the weight shifted. It settled again almost at once, but in the momentary chink it left, the

— 1 —

idea filtered through. I shall drown him. In absentia, necessarily. But just as effective as if he were here, as far as I need be concerned. A plan formulated. She kept moving, so that the midges should not settle. Hot and damp under her jacket, she could not expose more skin, she was searching now, her steps purposeful, to and fro along the tideline. She wasn't exactly sure what she was looking for until she found it: a roughly spherical lump of quartz, about an inch and a half across, still slightly jagged at one end, like a worn-down tooth. She picked it up.

I swear to God I shall put him behind me for evermore. This foolish temptation to turn for comfort to the torturer himself. Was any of it real? Did you love me at all? At all? So very foolish. I will never see him again on earth. She walked slowly back to the house, turning over the stone in her pocket.

She had done something to deserve all this. She had answered an advertisement. 'Master Mariner, aged fifty, seeks companion for long distance sailing. Own yacht. Searching for the wild and lonely places. No experience necessary.'

She had assumed he meant experience of sailing. A little of the other sort would have come in useful. A letter, a phone call, an arrangement to meet for lunch: 'I suggest the Merlin, in Morningside. I have been there before, with friends, and found it satisfactory. I want you to enjoy your lunch.'

She had enjoyed it. Just as well, because it meant missing a lecture that would have been important. 'You are a very attractive young woman,' he told her. And considering you're fifty, you're not so bad yourself, she thought, imagining that she was in control of the situation.

He kept his yacht at Aberdour. He would take her to see it. Unfortunately he was selling it.

'Selling it? I thought you wanted a crew?'

'Ah, but I'm buying another. A bigger one, for long voyages.'

'How far did you go in the one you had?'

'I was in Gib last year. The Medi.'

'How much further were you planning to go?'

'Tonga.'

Tonga? She looked it up on the map when she got home. Well, they certainly couldn't go further. 'Hadn't you better teach me to do it in the Firth of Forth first?' she had said.

'Oh, you'll soon learn.'

When she got back to the house above the beach, she took the stone out of her pocket, and put it on the desk. Then she took her wallet from the top drawer, and removed a small photo. It was of him, head and shoulders. It was so small because she had torn up every photo of him she had, the last time she had thrown him out, and she had only been able to salvage two complete heads from the dustbin, after she had forgiven him again.

The other head had already been put to use. She had sellotaped it to a sheet of paper, and drawn in his body, with large genitals. Then she had taken a packet of pins... .

My God that'll hurt him, if it works. It'll work all right, one way or another.

The picture with the pins in it was hidden in her desk. So now there was only one photo left. She tore off a piece of brown tape, and stuck the photo to the stone.

I am going to drown MacKail.

The day she had met him she had walked in the park, and counted seven magpies. Who wants secrets anyway? She thought he did, then. The second time they met, they had lunch in a basement café. He wore a blue seaman's cap. He liked to yarn about his days in the Merchant Navy. A captain of a tanker, that's what he'd been. Oil tankers take four miles to stop, or is it five? Such a responsibility. He'd been in the Royal Navy before that, working against drug smugglers trying to get into Singapore. Not that she approved of the Navy, or the oil industry. But he was so ingenuous. Then he'd been a pilot on the Ugli river, in India. After three years in India, he'd always thought he'd like to go back. Of course, she thought, he's far too old for me, out of another world. His politics are unsound. She invited him home for tea.

'I love you,' he said. 'I loved you as soon as I saw you.' He kissed her. 'I would love to make love to you.'

'Well, you can't.'

'Why not?'

Why not indeed? But we've only just met. That didn't sound very original. 'Well, you know why not.'

'No, I don't.'

'Well, we're not protected, are we? I don't want to get pregnant, or anything else.'

Could anyone be that innocent? This man could, apparently.

'When are we going sailing?'

When indeed? Here she was, months later, walking alone down the ness, and they had never been sailing yet. There was a good reason for this.

'That boat? Oh yes, he did buy a boat. He used to have picnics on it. Never took it out of the harbour. He was scared. He'd no idea what to do with it.'

'You mean he couldn't sail?'

'Never went sailing in his life.'

The sea was uncannily calm today, like milk. It was usually very clear, but today it was thick, opaque. Brown weed poked out along the edges, motionless. She crunched across a small pebbled beach with boats pulled up to the top of it. So much of her life had been spent walking along the shore. She knew the sea so well, from the land.

The day the news broke, there had been whales.

The first phone call came just before tea. It was the man from the Conservancy, asking if they could see whales in the voe. Someone had reported a sighting of pilot whales. If they got stuck in inland waters, they would lose all sense of direction, and throw themselves ashore by mistake. Their echo sound system would stop working, and they would commit a form of involuntary suicide. You would have expected them to evolve better than that. Outside with the binoculars, she had been the first to catch sight of them, down by the islands at the head of the voe. Black bodies surfacing, rising and dipping, swimming round and round, shining in the evening sun. Standing outside the porch, she and the others had passed the binoculars from hand to hand, watching.

The evening faded, and the whales swum aimlessly among the islands, trapped.

The second phone call came just before dusk. It was for her. Someone who knew what was happening had taken pity at last, and had plucked up the courage to tell her. He was not fifty. He was sixty-six. He had been married forty years. He had two children, her age. He had grandchildren. No, he had never been in the Navy in his life. At sea, yes, during the war. Possibly he got to be a mate. A compulsive liar. A cheat. A crook. Fraud. First forged his birth certificate years ago. Put ads like the one she'd seen in all the papers. Meeting women. No, he's lived in the islands most of his life. A no-gooder.

She stood at the window, clutching the phone. Listening. Unbelieving. Staring out at the voe. He had been going to join her. To meet the others here. Part of his holiday. Next week. Just then the whales turned. They came right past, under her very window. Huge gleaming bodies, knowing their way now, plunging together out into the open sea.

Once in a life-time you see something like that. She stared, open-mouthed. It will never happen again.

Dialling his number.

'Is that you, Andrew?'

'Yes?'

'I know about you now.'

'Oh.'

'Are you going to say you're sorry?'

A pause. 'I'm sorry it's over.'

'Is that all?'

'Yes.'

'Goodbye then. That's it.'

'Goodbye.'

Now, as she walked out towards the ness, the air began to clear a little. Ahead, under thick cloud, she could see a pale gleam of sun. The sea was like shells, chalk-white and serrated. The voe narrowed between the headlands, and in the midst of calm there was a ripple of tide. The water seemed to run both ways at once, in small whirlpools. He was evil. He loved me. He was evil. He did love me. There was some lost good in him. Something was real.

The blood test had been real. How many times has he done this? Who else does he go with? She was sick of people telling her she lived in the Aids capital of Europe. It took a week to get the result of the test. She took sleeping pills for six nights running, for the first time in her life. No one in the house knew about it. When the result came, she wept with relief, and realised in the same moment that had never been really what it was all about. A search for absolution, for purification. 'I feel as though I had been raped,' she told the doctor.

'Psychic rape,' he said. 'You were deceived. There is nothing wrong with you.'

I want a priest to bless me now. Holy water. To wipe his

stain away. You can't touch pitch…

She didn't believe in anything. She skirted the sea. The tide welled slowly upwards, without waves. Water surged round dry rocks with a gentle licking sound. The sea was like batter, beaten in a bowl.

My darling I love you I love you I love you There has never been anyone else No one that mattered There will never be anyone else If you reject me I will be alone for ever There is no one but you I was never in love like this before I have never known any woman like this You changed my life I love you I love you Nothing will ever be the same again Marry me Marry me I want to be married to you I want to buy a croft in the islands with you and live happily ever after

'I don't believe in marriage.'

'I can't give up my job.'

'I don't want children at this point in my life.'

'I have everything going for me. I'm not ready to retire yet.'

'But I love you.'

Oh the evenings spent explaining it all to him. 'What is this feminism you talk about?'

'Oh never mind. I'm too tired to explain. One day. Yes, one day I will. Let me live my life a bit first.'

'But I don't have so long. I want to spend the remainder of my life with you. I want nothing else.'

She didn't know if she could stomach that. But no one had ever offered her love like this in all her life. Such passion. Never had she felt so desirable, intelligent, attractive. The world was her oyster, and he was there to back her.

When he was there.

'I thought you were coming at three.'

'I was delayed at the university.'

'I could have seen a friend. It was important. I told her I had to get back, and then you didn't turn up.'

'I didn't say three for definite.'

She could see open water ahead now. The tide was making ripples at last, spreading out over the flat surface of the water. There were sounds. The wild call of a raingoose from the far side of the hill, then an answer, the same call back again from its mate at the top of the voe. Sheep bleated on the hill. There was the sound of water creeping up the shore. The cloud had lifted a little. The outer isles were dark brown, silhouetted on a thick horizon.

I am not defiled.

The pain under her ribs, where she kept the stone pressed tight, was not new. He had made her feel it many a time. She had been doubled over, as if the knife were really there, sitting on a bench in the park. 'You hurt me! You're hurting me!'

'Who are these men?'

'I've told you. There's nothing wrong with my life! There would be something wrong if someone as attractive as I am never had a boyfriend, I told you, I don't have any secrets. There's no one now but you.'

'How could I be faithful to you before I knew you existed?'

'I don't understand why you have had these men in your life.'

'You don't understand anything. You know nothing about life. You'd better go away.'

'I have never loved anyone but you. But I'm just another man to you.'

'For God's sake just go away.'

At which point he had left, for approximately twenty-four hours.

I can't really leave you I can't live without you I've tried but I can't Nothing like this has ever happened to me before please forgive me I love you so much I'm devastated I've been in hell please take me back I'm sorry I hurt you it will never happen again It's all right now It always will be Please take me back I can't bear it

She came to a small beach piled high with detritus from the sea. On the grass at the top she found a scabby man, a whole sea urchin. She rubbed off some of the spines. It was mostly purple, with white and pinkish mauve, unchipped. She put it carefully in her pocket, knowing it was pointless. She already had a fishbox full of driftwood, shells and stones. Some of it would end up in a flat in Edinburgh. Well, why not?

She sat down for a moment in the place where she had found the scabby man. Coltsfoot and tormentil studded the wet grass.

His wife, who had put up with petty crime for the last forty years, had now forgiven him this episode also, and had moved back in with him temporarily. Nothing like a bad man to attract a good woman. She brushed the midges off her eyelids. No chance of sitting still on a day like this. Her cheeks itched and flamed, and there were bites swelling on the backs of her hands. She got up hurriedly and walked on. There was no good in thinking of them, or pursuing their fortunes any further. He was out of her life forever. She would never set eyes on him again, except that she couldn't trust him not to lurk in the park hoping for a glimpse of her. After all, he had all day. There never had been a job, in the university or anywhere else. The last job he'd held down for a short time was as a hospital cleaner. She'd smelt the disinfectant on his hands once, and he told her he'd been spring-cleaning the bathroom. Two days ago she had checked out the university story.

'Good afternoon. Could I speak to Dr Miller in the Department of Oceanography?'

'I'm sorry, we don't have an oceanography department.'

'Oh. A student told me there was a Dr Miller, studying plankton. Would it be geography, zoology, or something like that?'

A pause.

'No, we have no Dr Miller. But the oceanography unit moved some years ago. You could try that. But I don't know where it went. Somewhere in the south. Shall I put you through to geography? You could ask.'

'No, no, that's all right, thank you. Thank you very much. Goodbye.'

She had actually come across the article in the *National Geographic* from which he'd lifted his story about research into plankton, and the effects of the hole in the ozone layer. She read it in the doctor's surgery, while she was waiting to hear her test result. She could scarcely concentrate, but it was all there. She recognised the names he'd dropped in her presence. He'd told her that when his research was finished he had the offer of running a project studying the movements of plankton in the Indian Ocean.

'With my naval experience and my degree, I'm just the man they want. You'd like India, I know you would.'

'Andrew, I'm not about to live in India. I have a job here.'

'I know you have your own life. Most women would want to be with their husbands. I know you're not like that.'

'No, I'm not.'

'But I won't go without you. I'd miss you too much. I'll give it up willingly for you.'

'You shouldn't do that. We can wait two years, if that's how long it is.'

'But it would be nice to have a little Andrew.'

'It might be a little Andrina.'

'Well, that would be nice too.'

Nice or not, every month she had waited in trepidation, and every month it had been all right. Neither of them had

been very responsible about birth control. She remarked
that he might not even be fertile, for all they knew. He said
nothing. Since he said he hadn't been with a woman for
fifteen years, there seemed little else to worry about. There
were moments when she was more than tempted by his
fantasies, closing her mind to the reality of an infant, which
would, from what she had observed, probably take at least
twenty years to grow up.

And some of them never grew up at all.

There was a touch like a faint breath on her cheek. Then
suddenly, wavelets splashed on the shore as if they had
fallen from the wake of an invisible craft. There was nothing out there, only a hint of a wind, and a blurring of lines
out to sea, like a scrumpled sheet of music. The ground was
rocky now, with patches of dead thrift between the lichened
stones, brown flowers stuck obstinately to dying stalks.
Across the voe, the hill was sloughing off its mist. The
heather was just coming out, staining the dead ground
purple. The sea shone like oyster shells.

What I am going to do is this: I have put the memory of
him, and all the pain, into this stone. I have held it to the
wound, like a hilt, and now the pain is in the stone. I have
stuck the photo to the stone. I have put brown sticky tape
over it, which means that I have looked at his face for the
last time. It was an attractive face, with blue eyes that
crinkled when he smiled, and broad weatherbeaten cheeks.
He had a very fair skin, that was always sore from shaving
until he started to let his beard grow. The beard was white
which made him look much older. But still I never guessed.
His nose was a bit squashed looking, but handsome in
profile. He looked exactly what he wasn't, a straightfor-
ward kind of chap, as he'd say himself. A bluff sailor. Such
clichés; now I see it, I trip over them whichever way I turn.
So — I am about to throw the stone, which is Andrew, as

far into this milky sea as I can chuck it. The sea is already full of skeletons, and all kinds of pollution. It will cope with this much better than I can. And everything that goes in there gets forgotten, sooner or later. I am going to organise a drowning, and then I will be free.

She had almost reached the point of the ness. The rocks were bigger here. The seaweed lifted and fell in a smooth swell, shining brown where the water left it gleaming. So my darling (for the last time) I am about to drown you.

The land gave out, and so she stopped. The chances were she would never go to sea now. No, she corrected herself, that need not be true. She had been sailing once since she met him. It was one of the times he had bullied her until she fled, and gone to stay with an old friend who had, as a matter of course, taken her for a sail in a lugger, round the harbour of the town where he lived.

'Take the tiller,' the friend had said, and vanished forward.

She held the tiller tight. It was all right at first, then the boat tilted, and tilted, and went on tilting.

'What do I do now?'

He looked up. 'Good God,' he said. 'Let go.'

The next day he had to go to work, and offered to lend her his car so she could drive around the island. 'Don't bash it.'

'Of course I won't. I know more about cars than I do about boats anyway.'

'Well, you certainly couldn't know less,' he said cheerfully.

She left for home after a long weekend, and he went back to preparing his yacht for a trip to the Lofoten Islands. She hadn't mentioned Andrew to him. He wouldn't have been interested. Relationships of that kind bored him. If he had wanted to, he could probably have sailed himself to Tonga. Really.

And only yesterday another friend, here, had offered to take her out fishing on the next good day. But no one would ever love her again. It was too late. She could never bear it. As for the sailing, maybe it was safer on dry land.

So, there had once been a man called Andrew MacKail who was a confidence trickster. He looked ingenuous, and pretended to come from the islands, two characteristics which were a great advantage to him in his criminal career. His forte was fraud and forgery. He could not manage without his wife, so every time that truly excellent woman left him, he put advertisements in the paper, seeking love nefariously. His plan with herself had been simple and sadistic. To make her give up her job, alienate her from her friends and family, get her pregnant, and then arrange to disappear, pretending he was off to India and would write to her. His only reason for doing this was to make himself feel powerful, since her life was a success, and his, to date, a resounding failure. What a sordid little story. She wondered if she could make it into a limerick:

There was an old man called MacKail
Who pretended he knew how to sail
A story which led
To him being in bed
With a woman who should have known better.

There wasn't time to think of a satisfactory ending, because the midges down here on the rocks were thicker than ever, hovering over the water like one of the plagues of Egypt.

In spite of them she clambered down over the rocks, her boots sliding over seaweed, then getting a purchase on white encrusted barnacles. She was below the tideline, where sea anemones gaped blindly, sucking on air between the waves. Water lifted and sighed round her feet, like a benediction.

Catharsis. The rocks shelved away steeply. The sea stirred, rose and fell around her peat-stained boots.

MacKail will die before I do, she thought. She might meet him in Purgatory, just passing one another. She was quite serious about that. Or, if Blake was right after all, they might find themselves together, crowding by that celestial river going down into the sea of life once more. There had been that moment of recognition when she met him. Of course, he had been practising, and she had been lonely. And his accent had made her feel at home, erroneously, for he was born in Abbeyhill, and the story of eviction from his island croft at the tender age of six was merely another tale. But in the final analysis, she did not distrust her intuition completely. It was possible there was a connection, not here, not now, not benign, certainly not romantic. It was equally possible that there was not. Belief was something that had to be accepted or rejected. Life was different. You had to take what you got, and survive it somehow.

A couple of gulls screamed overhead. Above them, the Loganair flight from the furthest island burred across the sky.

I commit my memory of you to the deep.

The sea was pale yellow under an unseen sun. She heard waves plash, and plash again, at different times along the ragged shore.

She took her stone in her hand, with the photo stuck to it, and threw for all she was worth.

There was a mild splash, a few yards out.

Done it. God please help me never to look that way again never never to think of him never to look that way again.

Fare forward, voyagers. The sea waits.

An Ugly Lover (tries to explain)

ANGELA MCSEVENEY

When you first claimed to love me
the shock had a violence
which thrilled through me.

Why should he think to say that?
but I have the nerve to question only your eyes
as I lie against you.

Nothing in me has been taught
to accept such a statement.

Believe me
I don't want to ignore you
but it would seem gall to reply.

Oh yes, I love you
but always I am wondering
what blow are you softening me for?

Where will it fall?

Smear Test

ANGELA MCSEVENEY

Left in the cubicle to my own devices
I examine the speculum.
It's bigger than I thought.

I fold towelling underwear
on top of a white petticoat
on top of canvas shoes.
It's Summer:
each waistband is sweat damp.

Nothing else for it:
I take off my body
and arrange it on the couch.

The doctor apologises that I had to wait,
warms the speculum under a hot tap.
I am not afraid. We chat.

I am prepared for the first touch of medical steel,
the next virginal loss.

Victim of Violence

ANGELA MCSEVENEY

The police issued a statement.

There had been people in the area
who must have heard her screaming.
Please could they come forward.

My address near enough was given
as the scene of the crime.

I checked for details down the newspaper column.

Yes, I'd been at home.
If I had only known to lean from my window
I could almost have seen it happen.

Nightmares plagued me.

I lay below leadweight sheets trying to rise.
I couldn't reach you.
I didn't hear you.

I pass by the spot every day:
a pretty place of mown grass, flowerbeds,
now as solemn as a well kept grave

and I hear you screaming.

Myself

ANGELA MCSEVENEY

I am the only souvenir I have
of you.

The walls took no interest.
They turned a blind eye
to all that went on within them.

The air holds no pictures of you:
only my tortured eyes can't let go
printing your image on everything.

I twist alone
in the aching space of a single bed
once crammed with the pair of us.

The mattress doesn't moan for you.

I can't let me forget
that we giggled as we made room
for my pushy breasts.

My skin harps on:
it can describe the entire length of you.

The sheets held only your scent.

Act of Union

A.L. Kennedy

WAITING HERE, with nothing to sit on — it was a bugger. You could sit, if you wanted, on the brick edge of the flower bed. But that would make you dirty; earth and chewing gum and that. Folk stubbed out their chewing gum on the bricks. It was disgusting.

Because of the rain, it was muddy this evening and she would have to watch herself more than usual, because she had on fawn slacks and the cream-coloured jacket. They were nice, but they showed the slightest thing and she liked to keep clean.

Later, she would be tired, but just now, she felt very settled and quiet inside. She was here. This was where she had run to. This wasn't away, this was here.

A block of faces came out to the sunlight, coats and hair rising in the breeze and she watched them. She knew how to watch.

Sometimes, there was a girl who was a dancer. This station must be near to where she lived. It was only a guess, but she ought to be a dancer. You could see in the way she walked, as though clothes were unnecessary. Very proud. She was too thin, but she had a lovely face and, if she was stripped bare naked she probably wouldn't look even a wee bit undressed. Her skin would be enough, better than clothes.

It would always be a good night if you saw her. The dancer was lucky.

The faces passed more quickly than you would think.

That was always the way. From the top of the steps until they reached her, she could count to seven slowly. Up to nine and they were beyond her, crossing the road and turning, going away.

No one had stopped this time. No one had really seen her, or hesitated. But they would. It was early, yet, and the dancer hadn't come.

It was funny how people could tell why she was waiting. In the way she could tell the dancer was a dancer. It was the same. Some people would see her waiting here and they would be able to tell.

At first, she had only noticed them, noticing her, and hadn't known why, or who they were. Now she could recognise all the types before they had moved from the shadow of the entrance and walked past the poster for young persons' travel cards.

Some of them did nothing. They looked at her or looked away, smiling, frowning, pretending she wasn't there. Some of them did what she needed. Not what she hoped, or wanted, just what she needed them to do.

By the time it was fully dark, the first one had come and gone. They had walked together to the car park and stayed in his car, without driving away. Then she walked back alone to the station and stood. She waited.

Twenty pounds, ten minutes. He had been English, which she preferred. Arabs had more money, but they frightened her. Scots were always somehow rougher, although she was Scottish too.

She was Scottish and here was London but it didn't make much of a difference, most people she met didn't seem to come from here. They were all strangers.

It did feel different, though. Out here, the houses were

all small with their own tiny gardens, too tiny to be useful. White walls and square, little windows looking over grass like green paper and stupid dots of flowers. The people walked past her in the street and didn't like her, but she wasn't sure of why that was. They might be able to tell that she was Scottish; they might not like the way she had to wait.

They should have been nicer to her really; she was only wee. And a stranger. Folk were dead unfriendly here.

Of course, this was a Friday night and the amateurs were out — just school kids making money for the weekend. She didn't like to wait near them. Soon she'd go into the station and ride to town. The town was more like Glasgow, like the city. Big, glass buildings and hamburger places and lights. Very bright, but very strange where the lights were and very black over everything else. She went between the two. The black to hide and the bright to show. The city was very suitable for what she did.

Going down the escalator, she passed the dancer. She looked tired.

The underground could be scary. Not because of people, because of itself. She didn't like the cold push of wind when the train came up to the platform. She didn't like the noises. Even in the Glasgow underground, which was small, she had been scared and this one was where that fire had been — all those people underground and burning — like the coal in old mines. She closed her eyes as the carriages slid beside her. They opened their doors.

MIND   THE   GAP

Sometimes, that was a tape-recording, but sometimes it was a person, trying to talk like a tape-recording, she'd noticed that.

Inside, when it started moving, she sat away from either end, in case there was a crash, or else she stood near a door and held on with her feet apart which made you more steady, even with heels.

She wasn't frightened often. Sometimes they would ask her if she was scared. Scared of them. If they wanted her to say so, she would tell them that she was, but she wasn't. For a person of her age, she was very brave.

The Hotel man had believed she was scared of him, but that was because she let him believe; that wasn't true, not really true. Also, she knew he would have to make her frightened, she knew he would like that a lot. For peace and quietness she let him think she was already scared.

She'd known he was like that from the beginning — breathing and looking at her and trying to make her afraid. He came to her room in the morning on the fifth day she was there and said she would have to pay her bill or go. He shouted and spoke about policemen and what they would do. Send her home, or lock her up and bodysearch her.

Locking her up would be better than home. The same, but better.

Whenever he spoke to her, the Hotel man breathed quickly, through his mouth. He looked at her and breathed in the way her mother had told her she ought to if she had onions to chop. If you breathed through your mouth, they wouldn't make you cry.

The Hotel Man breathed the way you should for chopping onions when he told her about the police and asked her about money and what could she suggest she ought to do. In her silences, he watched and breathed. Nobody cried.

She didn't cry then. And when she did, the following day, she was crying because of her mother, not because of him or being scared. She couldn't help crying, she was sad. She knew she would never be as good as her mother was now.

Her skin would never be as nice, nor her fingers so clever. She couldn't even cook, it didn't work. It didn't taste good. It wouldn't matter if she practised, there would always be something missing from what she did and she wouldn't be able to practise any more. Who would let her?

The Hotel Man was stupid. He was just satisfied with believing he'd made her cry. But he couldn't ever do that. She was too strong.

Coming up out of the station, the wind was rising, growing unpredictable. Different parts of a newspaper were diving and swinging in the air and there were whirls of smaller rubbish scraping the foot of the walls. It felt like something starting, maybe a hurricane again.

The last hurricane in London had come when she was still in Glasgow. In school, they'd had to write about it and she'd been sad because of all the ruined trees. Her father said there'd been a hurricane once in Glasgow, but nobody'd cared.

This had all been in the Autumn, after the third time she'd run to other places and before the fourth. The fourth time, she'd made it to London and the Hotel man.

He'd been like a father to her. Only he'd called it testing the goods when he did it and he'd made her take him out of herself and rub him. He'd put himself into her throat. Her father had been more sleekit. He'd climbed through the window from the street one afternoon and showed himself to her by accident on purpose.

Their sitting-room windows were opened right up and into the street and she could see other folk, by their windows, sitting on the pavement, standing in their rooms. Her father was wearing shorts and trainers, nothing else, and he sat astride the windowframe and smiled at her, let his shorts ride up. It didn't seem right. It didn't seem right to walk away from him without smiling back. It didn't seem right when he took her in the other room. It didn't seem right that all those people were there so close, just beyond the window.

Father called it having a cuddle and said it was her mother's fault. He'd used to do this with her mother but then she'd gone to somewhere else.

Doing it made you want to go somewhere else. You needed a different place to be. Then you got a different place and you were still wrong, because you were wanting a different time and to be a different person.

Of course this was payday Friday, end of the month, and that was always busy. After the fifth or sixth, she had a wee sit and something to eat. The gale was getting worse. It wasn't cold especially, but some of the gusts were so strong, when you faced them you couldn't breathe.

Watching through the plate-glass window with her coffee, she saw things becoming unsteady, losing control. It didn't feel dangerous now she was out of it, just very strange. Like being drunk without drinking.

She had her own choice of places to go for her quietness: chicken places, or pizza places, hamburger places, all kinds of places. She preferred to go where they sold doughnuts. Doughnuts had no smell. If you kept them in the napkin, your hands stayed clean and when you'd finished, your mouth was sweet.

Folk didn't mind a sweetness on your lips. If you smelled of grease and vinegar, you'd get nowhere. Not with the ones who noticed these things and those were the ones you should want.

She had seen women talking to men they met in the doughnut place, but you couldn't do that. You might not be let in again. She wouldn't do work here, anyway, this was her place, where she could rest. There might be one she would come in with who could have been her father or her uncle — one who had thought she looked hungry, or cold, or wanted feeding up. They would take her here and feed her, be her daddy for a while, and then they would take her away and be strangers again. The usual thing. She preferred to be here on her own.

A little crowd gusted in, on the way home from something, almost falling, hair wild, laughing. She smelled their mixture of perfumes, examined their clothes. One of the women looked at her and smiled, as the party sat down. One of the men next to her whispered and she turned away.

Along the wall and away from the window, there were boys in tracksuits, drinking coffee. You could tell they all knew each other, although they were sitting in groups around different tables. Once they were outside, they would get louder and walk together, filling the street. She didn't look at them and didn't avoid them, she just accepted they were there. You couldn't tell what people like that might do. You couldn't tell what a group of them might wait outside to do. They weren't bad; only curious. Afterwards, that made it feel worse; the way you had been their experiment.

Danny wouldn't be pleased about this; her sitting around on her arse all night and not making him money. And this week he needed a lot. He said he needed it for medicine, but she knew what kind of medicine that was.

She had nothing to do with that. Up at home, you were always getting offered that, anything, their mammy's tablets, anything, and she hadn't touched it then. It was fucking stupid. It made Danny stupid. He was just boring now. She could dress any way she wanted, he wouldn't care. He didn't even talk to her anymore, or eat the food she got. She tried to look after him properly, but he didn't want it, he only wanted the money, the medicine. He'd used to make love to her. He'd been different and really lovely. He'd used to hold her and kiss and say the nice places in Glasgow where they'd live.

They were going to go back home with their money. It would be great to go back with money, old enough to decide things and with money. She would have a baby, so they'd get a house, and she would take excellent care of it and call it James or maybe Mary, like her mother.

Now Danny was shooting up, she didn't want his child. She'd been so fucking careful, making people take precautions, trying so hard to make all of them take precautions, and he didn't know how hard that was and now he was sticking needles in himself. Sometimes she hoped he would just die. Sometimes she hoped they would all die.

The last of her coffee tasted sour and oily. She might as well leave it. It was all right to do that here. There were unfinished doughnuts and napkins, paper cups across most of the tables. The floor wasn't clean. Every now and then, a girl would come and clear things away. She looked bored and unhealthy, very pale. That was the kind of job you took when you couldn't get anything else.

Most of the staff here were black. She couldn't get over that. Every time you went to places here, the people who served you and cleaned up after you were black. It must be like this in South Africa.

The times when she thought of stopping it, of really doing something else, she always imagined having to work in here. If she was lucky, she would work in here. In two years time, she would be old enough to get a shitey, dirty job in here and work all week to earn what she could in a day, just now. Where was the sense in that? She knew she didn't get the money that she made. You didn't ever get the money, but you earned it, you were close to it, you knew it was yours.

And all these folk that wanted her to change and to take her away from this; they talked about qualifications and training and then they just stopped. Even they couldn't get it to make sense. They asked her what she wanted to do and then stopped, just lies or silence.

She knew what she was qualified for — she was qualified to fuck. That was all. Hand relief and oral or right inside you. They taught you that when you didn't want to learn it. They trained you. And they shouldn't do that. It wasn't right that she knew these things. She couldn't be normal now, only spoiled.

Something hard clattered against the window and birled away. It seemed to wake her from something. She'd been staring at the street without seeing for quite a while. Everything outside that could be was in flight, floating by, and it reminded her of looking at the Dentist's aquarium and of feeling scared over what was coming next.

It was past the time when she should be out there, too. Earn some more. But she felt a little feverish again, a little bit hot. If she bought another coffee and sat it would pass away. She hadn't felt right since she'd left the Hotel Man. Not since she'd had his present for going away.

A man in a nice jacket turned back from the counter and smiled. It was that daft, private smile you passed between two, always a little bit ugly, even if it was for you. The woman already at the table returned it with a shake of her head. A friendly, wee shake of her head. She was much younger than him. Probably he wouldn't mind if she was younger still. So many of them liked their girls little. Use them like women and treat them like weans.

Last night, a man like that had told her she should stop it and get out.

Not a man, a customer. He'd looked like a Social Worker when you saw him up close: the same kind of sad and tired, pathetic face. Trying to understand, as if he was the only one that could.

She'd got in his car as usual and then known he was weird. He was too relaxed. There wasn't much you could do with the weird ones, except to wait and see. He'd seemed harmless.

He'd told her he would pay her, but he didn't want anything. She told him that nobody didn't want anything. He just patted her knee and smiled.

'I made that myself. It has two secret drawers in it and a secret panel.'

He'd grinned and passed her a heavy, wooden box, with a sloping lid. The wood was pale with little pieces of darker wood, set in. She'd like the smell of it, and the smoothness.

She shouldn't ever let them take her home. Not take her anywhere unknown, because that wasn't safe. But she let him drive her to his home and take her in. He made her steak and beans and baked potato, because that's what she felt like asking for. He gave her wine, when she'd asked for voddy, but she drank it. Then he gave her the box.

'See if you can find the drawers.'

'I'm not a kid.'

'O.K. Don't. I've got a video I want to watch. If you don't mind.'

'You don't sleep, then.'

'Not too much. And I want to see this film. Then you can tell me all about yourself.'

He smiled, as if that was a funny thing to say.

When she woke up, he was looking at her. He told her she must have been tired and she nodded. The T.V. wasn't on, which meant he must have been watching her, instead of the video. That felt odd.

'You're not too well, are you? Do you know why?'

She shook her head, just a little, thinking that of course she knew why. She didn't eat well, or sleep enough, or live in a nice flat like his. She wasn't well because of the rats and damp and filthiness in Danny's squat, because there wasn't a toilet there, not even water to wash.

The man kept on looking at her. You could see he was concentrating on being kind, on letting her talk.

She wasn't going to tell him anything. It was none of his business, not even if he had paid for her time. Was this him trying to check if she had V.D.? Well, she was due for it again, but she was clean, just now, so he didn't have to worry about that.

'Don't you think you deserve a bit better than this? Someone your age? You shouldn't be stuck with this. You need a future.'

No she did not. A future? All that time, all the same? She didn't need that. Or deserve it.

'I'm nineteen, I can do what I like.'

'I didn't ask how old you were. I could tell you how old I think you are. Maybe fifteen. I could tell you how much older you already look, but you know that.'

She watched him think of something else to say.

'You're not from round here. Where are you from?'

Maybe if she lifted her skirt that would shut him up. Then he wouldn't feel sorry for her. Then he'd stop trying so hard to respect her. She wasn't worth it. The Hotel Man had shown her that.

When he'd found out she was leaving him, he'd locked her in her room. She'd been there for almost a day when he took her down to where the boilers were. It was night and the hotel above her was quiet. The men sitting round the walls were also quiet, drinking, waiting for her. The Hotel Man did it first, and then he left.

It was maybe the following afternoon when she knew he'd come back again. Except she was in a different place then, in her room on top of the bed. She was so dirty, stiff with their dirtiness.

He told her she had half an hour to leave.

'Now you can go, because I've decided you're going. I've had all the use out of you I'm gonny get. Now you're nae use, so you're out. You're nothing, but I think you know that now. If you don't, you'll soon find out. You'd better. Hauf an hour, cunt. And you're out.'

She looked along the couch at the man. He was still staring at her.

'I've got nothing to tell you. Would you like me to go?'

'No, that's all right. Now you're here, you might as well stay.'

When they'd finished he brought sheets and stuff to the sofa. He tucked her in. Well, she hadn't expected he'd let her sleep in his bed. She wasn't clean. But he kissed her a lot, on the stomach, on the mouth.

In the morning, he gave her cereal and toast for breakfast and coffee which she didn't drink. She didn't let him drive her back, because she felt sad again and that should be private. When she left, he squeezed her hand and watched until she'd turned the corner of the street. She wished he'd just go away.

It had taken her hours to walk back to town. Danny hadn't been there when she got in and it was better without him. She knew that she wanted to stay where she was and have Danny go somewhere else. That would make her lonely, but it would be best.

With the money that she'd kept from Danny and what she'd

earned tonight, she could go back home. She could go up for a while and stay and then come back. Sometimes she felt really homesick, but she couldn't go to live back there. She wouldn't do this in Glasgow, only here, so she could only stay for a short while and then come back, because you had to work. You had a chance if you were working.

Perhaps she would go for a trip soon. Now it was the Year of Culture. You kept seeing posters about that. Things must have got better there and she should go.

She thought she wasn't feeling too bad now and she might as well get started again. As she stepped out to the pavement and the wind took the door from her hand, she remembered how good it had been at first to go in and buy her own meals in places like this. She had known she could go by herself, whenever she wanted, and then choose whatever she liked. At the time, it had felt like independence.

A Wee Tatty

ALISON KERMACK

HE GOAT the idea offy the telly. Heard oan the news this Chinese boy hud ritten 2 000 characters oan a singul grainy rice. Well o coarse, he kidny rite Chinese an he dooted if thur wiz any rice in the hoose (unless mebby in the chinky cartons fi last nite). Butty liked the idea. Whit wi the asbestos fi wurk damajin his lungs an him oan the invalidity an that. Well. He hudda loatty time tay himsel an no much munny ti day anyhin wi it. Anny didny reckon he hud long tay go noo. It wid be nice, yi ken, jist tay day sumhin tay leeve sumhin behind that peepul wid mebby notice. Jist a wee thing.

So wunce the bairnz wur offty skule an the wife wiz offty wurk, he cleared the kitchin table an hud a luke in the cubburds. Rite enuff, nay rice. He foond sum tattys but. Thottyd better scrub thum furst so he did. Then took thum back tay the table. He picked the smollist wun soze it wizny like he wiz cheatin too much, anny began tay rite oan it wi a byro.

He stied ther aw day. Kept on gawn, rackiniz brains an straynin tay keepiz hand fi shaykin. Efter 7 oors o solid con-sen-tray-shun, he ran ooty space. Heed manijd tay rite 258 swayr wurds oan the wee tatty. He sat back tay huv a luke. Even tho heed scrubd it, it wiz still a bit durty-lukin an it wiz that fully ize yi kidny see the rytin very well. Bit still. He felt heed acheeved sumhin. He wiz fuckn nackert. He laydiz heed doon oan the table an fella sleep. He didny wake up.

When his wife goat back fi hur wurk, she foond the boady lyin it the table. She gret a wee bit but theyd bin expectin it. She pickt him up an, strugglin under the wait, tryd tay shiftim inty the back bedroom. Haff way throo it goat tay much furrur an she hud tay leevim in the loabby til she goat a naybur tay helpur.

Wunce she goatim throo the back, she sat doon it the table an thot aboot how tay tell the bairnz. Mebby efter thur tea. Aw kryst, haff foar, she better pit the tea oan. Thursday so thur wizny much in the hoose. She noticed the tattys oan the table an thot it wiz nice o hur man tay scrub thum furrur. She chopped thum up an pit thum oan tay bile.

That nite, even tho the bairnz didny notice, the tiny drop o ink made the stovyz tayst that wee bit diffrint.

The Shadow Minister

ALISON KERMACK

by meenzy a contrapshun
lyk a perryscoap
wi a tellyscoap
attachd tay it
   whyl cashully stroallin
   aloang downin street
ah chansd tay luke
in the upper windy
i nummer ten

ah seen the pee ehm
sittin inna big arrumchayr
in frunty a big coal fyr
hoaldin a mappy scoatlin
oan the endy a toast foark

funny thing wiz
   thoa ah kidny see it say cleerly
   kiz it happind tay faw
   oan the oappisit waw
the shaddy i the pee ehm
wiz dayn igzackly
the saym thing

The Bogey Man

ALISON KERMACK

he sezees a gid man
bit…

he
hurts yi
if yi dinny day
whit yir telt

he
keeks at yi
throo a seekrit wee peephoal
when yir oan the lavvy

he
gets inty yir hed
an wochiz yur thinkin
He mayks yi pritend
heez yur dad
an yi hufty olwaze
be gid aw the time
kizzif yur no

he
throze yi inty
a grate big fyur
til yur aw burnd up

Scott's Porrij

ALISON KERMACK

ahm noa big fanny
porrij masel
butta bottit fur the bernz
kizzit sayd
thur wizza free gift
inside

turnz oot
the free gift
wizza wee plastic modul
oah nyooklur powur stayshun

now tell me
whittir ma bernz
gonny do
wi that?

smooth

JANICE GALLOWAY

THE FROCK was wet at the neck.

The good frock.

She tried to suck the satin rim to see what sort of wet it was.
Gin might stain it, the salt from her face would leave marks.
It wasn't machine-washable. But her mouth wouldn't reach.
Not properly. Jesus jesus. She couldn't feel her mouth
properly. Too swollen and frayed. It was most probably
bruised from rubbing and chewing, her teeth scoring into
the soft inner lining, all those close-to-the-surface veins. It
would be red in there, penis-tip purple. Her nose felt broken
and squashy too, the vessels in her eyes lumpy. Like tuber
roots. And still running, tracking the wet down the numb
shape where her face had been. They felt more real on the
way down her neck and over the breastbone. Stopping at the
rim of cloth. It was a nice dress, low-cut and flattering. Ha.
It would definitely stain. And crush, it would crush to hell.
Serve her right. She deserved all she got. Believing it like
that, the idea of believing at all. That the man could ever
have meant such a thing, that perfectly beautiful man saying
what he had said, that he was

She couldn't even think the words. It was too embarrassing.
The word marriage in that foreign mouth and her taking it
all in that he was prepared to

But then again, Luca wasn't entirely sane.

It struck her so suddenly her mouth fell open.

It struck her so suddenly she felt slapped and that was probably a good thing. Slapping people stopped them being hysterical. She certainly should be slapped if this was the kind of thing she believed: the promise of a man who was not entirely jesuschrist almighty what sort of woman did that? A stupid bitch, that's what kind of woman did that. The kind who just wanted to hear things that flattered her vanity. Just to hear him say it. Believing it though, it was the believing it, the terrible vanity of the thing. She was to blame for that. Horribly to blame. And this was what happened if you made that kind of mistake, allowed that kind of self-aggrandizement its way in. God never gave you a break at all, the bastard. Just never gave you a break. The frock rustled as she turned onto her back, spreadeagled over the cushions. Crushing to fuck. Served her right. If it wasn't so funny it would be

HA

HAHA

Giggling in an ironic way made your chest sore, though. A kind of stabbing pain under the right breast. But she wouldn't touch her breast. It would be too tragic. She couldn't stand to touch her breast. She leaned back instead, feeling the give of springs under her spine, this sofa he had lain on her with and talked about himself when she had found him a thing of beauty and a joy forever, a true thing. She had found him a true thing because because because

It didn't bear thinking about, the because.

It didn't bear thinking about at all.

She swallowed what was left in the glass, that was what was left of the bottle liking the way it caught and hurt in the back of her throat and curled herself deeper inside the sofa cushions, hand up to the nape of her own neck. Something he had done. He used to clear her hair aside to put his mouth there, settle his lips and kiss but only lightly (he only ever kissed lightly) her own hand feeling the nape of her own neck and the hair she had washed despite the fact that she was not going anywhere and there was no-one to see it: wiping it away from the skin over and over with the same sweep of the hand. Her scented hair, washed for no-one and feeling uselessly like silk like

velvet like

something someone could

Why did he not want

her own hand

her own neck

her beautiful smooth hair

The material screamed into the cushions. One of the net petticoats was tearing. Her throat hurting with finished gin stroking this perfect smoothness, this thing she had made from inside her own body. The thing he didn't want any more.

Hair separates from the scalp with a sensation of burning.

When there is no more drink to hand, you think of something. You manage as best you can.

Aliens

LINDA MCCANN

That morning as my banister uncurled
I stroked a wound 'Black Bastards Go Home.'
White-knuckled, swastika letters,
Newly knifed, but like an old woodcut.
They would love to carve it in a brown arm.
Sandpapering, I thought
They'll argue anything these people —
Except that black is white.
But as the words powdered and blew away
I saw I had more to do
For under the varnish and the stain
All the wood was white.

Tom Leonard's Good Night

Linda McCann

Mr Greeting-Face, Mr Testy,
Mr World's-Weight-on-Shoulders,
Unanimous hands lift and push,
submerge him into a black taxi,
shut the door along with him.
Like a cork, up he bobs again
stuck half-through the window,
telling us another thing.
I hug him, shout 'I love you Tom.'
The taxi moves. He watches me,
near-sober, lost for abuse. Roars
'I don't fuckin deserve it then.'

The Cockney Piper

Alison Armstrong

IT'S SO COLD in here — the school forgets to leave on the heating for the evening classes. I can feel my skin pores tightening to conserve heat, and my body shrinks from the touch of my chilly blouse. Soon, though, my skin will be insensitive and impenetrable — a barrier against *them*.

I don't want to face them tonight — I'm too tired. Most teachers would give their right arm for a class of OAPs and others, who are taking Higher English for the pure pleasure of books. The OAPs are no problem — they pass the exam and die happy. It's the others who always trouble me; they're odd, and whatever they say, they aren't here for simple bookish pleasure. My guess is that education's the sticky tape and string that's holding their minds together. Take Cameron. Perhaps he needs the routine of study and attendance to stay this side of sanity, or perhaps there's something about me that compels him … Hell, I'm a lecturer, not a social worker. I don't know what he wants.

Here he comes now, the clump of his big feet drowning the distorted echo of other feet and voices. Funny how these echoes express a building's emptiness more than silence. It's like being inside a dead thing, with sightless black windows for eyes. Only Cameron is alive, in a maniacal, destructive way. He's come to suck my blood.

'I amna fou' sae muckle as tired — deid dune.' Yes, that's me. But where do I go from here? I can't run tonight's class on the subject of my own inertia. Understanding these verses would help, but the language is impossible. The class — or rather Cameron — chose to study MacDiarmid, and I was wrong to let him choose. We should be doing something like Wordsworth, or even Donne — something I could control. MacDiarmid was a big mistake.

Cameron and the rest are here now — Cameron striding in while the others creep. As usual, he gives me the briefest of nods, and settles himself so his back is turned towards me. I bet he's SNP. He wants to vanquish me tonight, so I'll slink back to England to think again before I try to teach the Scots their heritage. But despite Cameron, I must continue. It's my job. A sahib must act like a sahib.

'Good evening,' I begin, tactfully calling the class to order. The OAPs wait respectfully, conditioned by the sanctity of Queen's English, and memories of the dominie with his belt. But Cameron is listening to music on his personal stereo, until his neighbour gives him a nudge. He then has to disentangle the lead from his hair, pack the equipment away and ferret in his bag for books and papers. All this takes time, and some of the OAPs are becoming anxious.

'Take your time, Cameron,' I say to pacify matters. 'We'll begin and you can join us when you're ready.'

'I'm sorry about the cold in here,' I continue, turning to the rest of the group. 'We'll just have to make the best of things. Keep your coats on if you think you'll feel the chill.'

Those who've already removed their coats hasten to put them on again. They're like sheep, these people. They understand the concept of command, or prohibition, but not the concept of suggestion. It's the result of a lifetime's skivvying, but it's hardly a sound intellectual basis for an English course. Cameron, on the other hand, isn't docile enough. He suffers from an incurable hatred of conformity, which is a shame, because he's damned intelligent. But who wants a forty year old washed-up rebel?

Final checks before I start the session. Can everyone see a book? Yes. Some OAPs are dutifully sharing library books, and Cameron is busy thumbing through a dog-eared copy of his own. Pens? Paper? Everyone is well supplied. The cold is tolerable now, and my shell, my exoskeleton is hardening, so I'm safe. MacDiarmid here we come.

'Last session, we decided we'd look at Hugh MacDiarmid's "A Drunk Man Looks at the Thistle."' They nod, silently, in agreement, because it never occurs to them to dissent. Their passive signals reassure me, and I carry on. 'Now, you sit your Prelims shortly, so we won't have time to read it all. But I want you to have *some* poetry in your files before the exam. The broader your range, the better equipped you'll be.'

I'm delaying the start, with all this hogwash about exams. Cameron knows what I'm doing. He's turned in his seat to face me, and is watching me through narrowed eyes. He can read me like a book and he's challenging me now, daring me to fling myself headlong into the trap he's set. 'Just some background before we begin,' I remark, trying to sound casual, fumbling for my notes. 'It was published in 1926 and it represents a series of metaphysical —'

'Metaphysical balls,' interjects Cameron. 'It's about colonialism. Listen.'

He reads:

'"I micht ha'e been contentit wi' the rose

Gin I'd had only reason to suppose

That what the English dae can e'er mak guid

For what Scots dinna —"'

(How fragile is my shell. I can feel it ready to shatter under this assault, leaving me raw and bleeding. If I hug myself — thus — I might just stay intact. This attack of Cameron's is flawed and clumsy, and I think it's just intended to unnerve me. I'll be all right if I can counter with a more subtle argument. But he reads beautifully.)

'"— … and a'e threid

O't drew frae Scotland a' that it could need.

And left the maist o' Scotland fallow."

There's your proof. The leeching English rose sucking the lifeblood of Scotland.'

He slaps his book down on the desk, open, with its spine uppermost. Having made his move, he sits back in triumph and waits for me to make mine. He's in my direct line of vision now, that long, lanky body uncoiled and at ease. Soon, he'll be ready to strike again.

His rudeness has distressed the OAPs, and they're dithering like pigeons cooped up with a snake. I suspect that some have grasped who the English Rose is supposed to be, and they're all looking to me to save the situation.

I smile. 'Thanks Cameron. I'm glad you've been reading ahead. But surely there's more to "A Drunk Man" than nationalistic grievance?'

'Perhaps. Aye.' He didn't expect me to rally, and now he's beating a tactical retreat. I pursue my advantage.

'In fact, I started to say that "A Drunk Man" was described as' — I fumble for my notes again — 'a series of metaphysical pictures of Scotland and the Scottish psyche. MacDiarmid himself wrote those words. So here we have an explanation of the work straight from the author. But what does he *mean*?'

I ask the closing question in a tone of weighty significance. It's an adroit move. I've just recaptured command of the intellectual high ground and at the same time, I've shifted the attention away from Cameron. All the OAPs — and Cameron — are sunk deep in thought. If I'm lucky, this question could occupy them for the entire evening.

One old lady has her hand raised. 'What does "meta-physical" mean?' she asks timidly. In the background Cameron 'tuts' impatiently, and the lady shrivels. My OAPs need protecting.

'That's a very good question.' The old lady blushes with embarrassed pleasure — I've restored her self-esteem. 'In fact, it's a difficult question to answer because "metaphysical" is hard to define. It can mean the process whereby ordinary things express extraordinary ideas. In "A Drunk Man", we'll see how the thistle becomes a metaphor for Scottish manhood. We're observing the way a mind changes and builds associations, expanding to great themes from small beginnings.'

Jesus, I'm on form tonight. I thought I didn't understand what was happening in these Godforsaken verses. I thought I didn't know what metaphysical meant, either. Amazing what you can pull out of the hat when your back's against the wall.

'And ten to wan the piper is a Cockney.' They're dancing to my tune now, busily scribbling down what I've just said. Even those shaggy, curly locks of Cameron's are bent industriously over the paper. He still has a full head of hair, and there's no sign of grey amid the dark auburn. He looks ten years younger than his real age — it's quite remarkable, given the private hell he's rumoured to have gone through. Perhaps that's kept him away from the ageing effects of a proper job. I wonder if it's wise to ask him what he thinks about metaphysical. I'd be disturbing him, but if I don't ask him, he'll probably volunteer the information on his own terms. And that could be a disaster. 'What do *you* think metaphysical means, Cameron?' I enquire.

He looks up, sweeps his hair away from his face and glares at me shrewdly. 'Means?' he says at last. 'How?'

'What's metaphysical about these poems we're studying,

in your opinion?' Explanation is a mistake. Cameron hasn't asked for clarification to enlighten himself, but to discomfort me.

'In my opinion ...' he drawls softly, then stops. 'No, it's got nothing to do with my opinion. It's *your* opinion you're after.'

He goes beyond mere rudeness. He's a threat, and there's some reason why I have to fear him that has nothing to do with this classroom. It's something in my mind — a vivid feeling I can't identify. It has to have a foundation, but what? 'Okay,' I assume the harassed teacher's weary patience. 'How do *you* interpret *my* opinion?'

'In your opinion' — he glances at the notes he made — 'in your opinion, metaphysical means he can say anything he likes.' He watches me for my reaction, and repeats softly: 'Anything.'

This isn't my opinion; at least, this isn't the way I expected it to be interpreted. If this enquiry is leading me anywhere, it's leading me back into danger. My arms hug my body, and I cultivate an interested frown. Leaning forward, I ask, 'What do you mean?'

'Freedom. It's because he's fou' — that means he's drunk. He'd have the same freedom if he was — ' here he pauses and says in a low voice — 'mad.'

Mad. And we're alone in this building with him. He's said it — now it's open. Anything could happen. The OAPs are fluttering feebly like limed songbirds, but the power, the tension, in this room, comes nowhere near *them*. It's held in the direct line of our glance. Cameron holds me without blinking, and will not let go. A madman looks at the rose.

His posture belies the tautness of the situation. He's rocking back in his chair, and is stretching to his full length. His sweater has risen above his belly, exposing taut flesh covered with a reddish down. I've seen this before. I don't want to remember what happened, but I'm forced to. It's all there, in the dream I had.

My dream happened in the colours of a sunny day, but the colours were abnormally intense. His red hair burned in the evening sun as he wheeled me away in some pram-like contraption. I made no protest. We were going into the night — I know because suddenly everything faded to a dim pastel, as if covered by a cobweb.

There were pursuers — I don't know their identity, but the infallible logic of dreams made me sense them in the urgency of our flight. Of course I wanted to be found in time, but I'm assuming that now. It wasn't in the dream. Where that wish should have been, there are confused desires that I'm ashamed to recognise.

'Mad,' I repeat aloud. 'Fou', like Foolish. Letting go of reason so the mind can see things it doesn't otherwise perceive. Yes, you're right.' Everybody makes notes, but only Cameron understands what I'm saying. I could add, 'like dreams,' but there's no need. He knows I've realised; knows I can no longer fight what's been there all the time. In the dark shack where he took me, I felt his hair falling onto my face, the way it falls onto the paper when he writes. I saw his belly as I see it now, only then it was virgin-white in the blackness. It came against mine and retreated, forward and back, forward and back. It felt wonderful — The thistle and the rose, both enjoying the struggle. Made for each other.

It's deeply embarrassing. Just looking at him now is making me blush and I've broken out in a sweat. The silky material of this blouse doesn't absorb perspiration and the moisture will dry on me and chill me to the bone. Am I hot? Or cold? I can't claim I'm hot when conditions here are freezing — they'd take me for a weirdo. Like Cameron. He's got my soul and he'll keep it if I don't do something. I can't disintegrate in front of all these people.

'Prelims.' The pedagogic apparatus maintains unity, like tough enamel on a crumbling tooth. 'Time passes. We could spend all night discussing general principles, but you need specific references to get you through the exam.' The OAPs look at me, masks with no individual names: the Chorus. They'll get through the exam; they don't deserve to fail. And Cameron? To pass exams you need orthodoxy and he hasn't got it. I'll have to fail him, it's my job. It's also my prerogative.

He has his head bent over his book now, but he's watching me from behind the tangles of his hair.

'"They're nocht but zoologically men,"' I quote ineptly. 'This evening, I want you to tell me who "they" are. Also' — I say this carefully — 'what has diminished their manhood?'

If I met his eyes now, I'll see history. Defeat perhaps; hatred almost certainly. But now I've begun the lesson, none of this matters. Cameron is no longer a threat. He's nothing.

Rosie

Mary McCann

Here is a girl, Rosie, she's thirteen. She's going to the sea bathing pool, and it's a heatwave. A scorcher, as her mother calls it. Often it's grey, with soft rain, or grey with a high wind and white waves, but today it's blue. Blue is the predominant colour, sky and sea. Heatwaves are rare here in southwest Scotland with all that Atlantic weather, wind and rain all the way from America. You can't see America, she thinks, only Arran. America is sort of there nonetheless, a presence beyond the horizon, far far away, far beyond green low Ireland that she's seen from the Ardrossan to Belfast ferry. America, land of glamour. Has she started collecting filmstar cards yet? Mitzi Gaynor, Susan Hayward, Jayne Alison? With their dazzling lipstick smiles and their taut bosoms in deep cut, crossover silk dresses? She will soon, that's for sure. But in the meantime it's school holidays and a heatwave. Dad must let her off painting the house today, maybe everyone recognises the perfection of it, the heat bursting up off the pavements, the promise of the sea water warming at last, sunbathing without goose-pimples, that Continental feeling. Not that she's ever been to the continent but everyone knows how it's done. Sunglasses, towels, glamorous tans. She will let her salty hair dry in the sun today, hoping for a transformation, mouse to gold, gold to white blonde, blonde the ultimate, the head turner, stardom. She breathes in the salty air, full of hope, happy to be alive, bouncing down the road in the sun.

In the damp dark changing cubicle at the shabby old pool she pulls out her costume from her towel roll and drags it on, wriggling to get it up her body and tie the straps behind her neck. It feels soft and light, thin cotton sewn in little quilted squares with elastic thread, shirred more tightly in a band above and below her waist so it pulls her in. She looks down and sees her soft breasts, which seem to be getting larger by the month, held in the cotton, but not properly, not as if it was a bra. They bounce a little as she moves. She makes a face. She longs for a bra for everyday and a swimsuit with proper bra cups like other girls'. Her mother seems to be blind and deaf to her need even though Rosie asks her often. Sally who came to school every summer when the fair turned up in town, had an amazing costume with bones. She wore it at primary school swimming lessons; with her gold earrings and her smudgy eyes tired from working in the fairground at night and her sophisticated pointy bosom she looked at least fifteen. Not fair. This cotton swimsuit, dark blue and red flowery cotton, it's a child's one. Rosie sighs. There's a horrible feeling when people look at you in your swimsuit, you don't know what you look like, you might have a huge wobbly bottom or knobbly knees or be showing something you shouldn't. And she's worried she's fat, her stomach is round, it keeps getting rounder. A wave of fear comes over her, hard to name, a wide boundless fear containing the question *am I all right, will I pass?* and the huge lonely responsibility of it all, having a body and being no one else but yourself, no escape.

She sighs again. Then she recalls that it's early in the day and the pool is quiet. She'll be able to get in the water without too many folk watching; and she loves swimming. Suddenly she can't wait to swim, grabs her wire clothes basket, swishes her curtain aside, takes a few steps to the counter and pushes the basket over it to the woman attendant. 'Right hen,' says this person, '29,' clonking the basket into a numbered hidey hole. '29, thanks,' says Rosie, '29, 29,' memorising her number, feeling light and free, swinging down the corridor to the pool exit.

Here's an open space, and a club changing room, a weighing machine, a mangle for wet costumes, a cold shower, hose pipes and paraphernalia, and a full-length mirror. Rosie walks out of the gloom towards a brilliant white oblong doorway on the far side of the mirror. Aware of movement in the mirror she stops and glances in. And sees, just for a minute, a stranger, standing in the light from the door, a tall brown-haired girl with large blue eyes in a concentrated stare, a long body in a pretty blue and red bathing suit, white arms and legs. Her body is both thick and slim, her knees, hands and feet large but strong. She looks balanced and capable. Even her breasts look nice, she could be wearing a stick-out bra for all you could tell. Rosie looks again, amazed. It's me, she thinks. She moves herself round and twists back to try and see her bottom. It is big but it doesn't look out of proportion really. Her heart lifts. I'm not bad, she thinks. A great sigh of gratitude and relief. And walks on into the light, out on to the newly white-washed concrete, across to the pool with the light blazing, the pavement burning her bare feet, the light off white cement and blue water going right into her and through her, as if she is a new kind of creature that can live in this new bright world. And she puts her foot in the brilliant water and it's warm. It's just perfect.

Lowdown

LINDSAY MCKRELL

I feel like a reptile
no zest
no smile
not hip
no style
nothing else to say
I eat a lot
don't do a lot
One of those bad days.

Taste

ALISON CAMPBELL

Tongue's membranes throbbing with fiery pickaxes.
Lime chutney
Hot pepper sauce
Peach relish
Mango pickle
Spread on
Crawford's Butter Puffs.
Goa meets Glasgow.

I throw over nine chillies in my curries.
Spoons mounding with turmeric and garam masala
Fast sand filling black holes of oil
Amongst the onions and coarse black pepper.

A legacy of a bland childhood,
Spicy food is my latest
Undoing.

Widdershins

Janet Paisley

An wha's tae say ah wis wrang? Ah seen thum thegither. Ah seen thum go in the pub, an it Wednesday. An ah'd seen thum afore. Doon the Steckie whin awbody else wis workin. He wis haudin hur fit. Haudin it up an dryin it oan a white hankie. An hur sittin leanin back oan the bank wi hur leg, shinin wet fae the watter, streeched up tae him an hur fit airched in his haun. Ah seen thum.

Ah clattert the poats an pans the nicht, steerin masell up, ye'll ken. There wis nuthin else fur it bit tae tell him. He wis huvin a bit read o the paper, wi his bitts aff an the damp stull steamin oot his soaks it the fire. Ah went ben an riddled the coals.

'Mither,' he says. 'Ye'll be gaun doon through that grate the noo if ye dinnae caw caunny. Whit's up wi ye?'

'Me,' says I. 'Whit wid be up wi me?' He shiftit in his sate an the paper fell ower oan itsell.

'Weel, ye'll be seein daylicht through they pats the morra,' he says. 'Fur ah doot ye've left a bottum in thum. Ye're nivir this het up ower a couple pun o berries?'

'Naw, ah'm no. Though ah pued thum masell, mind. Bit ah'll hae burnt worse than some wild rasps in ma time, nae doot.' Ah draw braith. 'It's your Ellen hus goat ma heid burlin.' There, it wis oot an his chin comes furrit, jist like his faither's yaised tae, wi his broos doon.

'Whey's that?' he says, thin like. So ah tell him. Wednesday, whin she disnae work Wednesday. An doon the Steckie this efternin, paddlin like bairns an drying each ither. Ye kin tell a loat fae a touch. He flung the paper oan the flair an goat up.

'Ye're no gaun doon there,' says I. He's pittin his bitts oan, no even his guid shune. An ah ken whit he sees. Donald's flat abin the pub, an the twa o thum up there. Alane. Thegither. The waw shakes wi the door shuttin it his back. It's a wunner the gless is stull hale.

An it's no jist ma heid that's burlin. Ma stomach's cawin roon, fair hoat an jumpin. Goad gie him the patience tae fund oot whit he needs tae fund oot, an lit him keep his temper. Ah kent she wid nivir be guid fur him. There's no a man passes hur withoot lukin. See it in the wey she walks. Like a cat, aw smooth an flowin. Queenin it. Bit she'll no ful a Cameron laddie. Ah'll see tae that.

The waitin kills me, an ah huv tae wait. The daurk's creepin in an feet comin hame rattle the quate. Bit nivir a fit oan oor path, nivir a scrape oan the step. Ah staun it till ah kin staun it nae mair, pit a scarf ower ma heid an go oot intae the street. It seems a lang wey doon the road tae the pub, an awbody's in thur beds, an it the only licht that's stull shinin.

The door openin cuts a bricht wedge oot the daurk an they're there, the twa o thum, no ten fit awa an Sandy's airm roon hur shouders. She flicks hur hair tae wan side an luks up it him.

'Ye've bin fetcht,' she says an goes tae step sideweys awa fae him. He disnae lit go, draws hur back wi his airm stull roon hur shouder. His een ur orange in the street licht. The fire in ma stomach turns tae chips o ice.

'Ah'm steyin it Ellen's,' he says. 'Ah'll git ma stuff the morra.'

'Ye micht wait till ye're wed,' ah say. 'Fowk'll talk.' He smirks, an it isnae a laugh. His vice is cauld, cauld.

'They wur checkin the stock,' he says. 'There's talk fur ye.' They baith turn awa.

Bit there's stull the Steckie. Ah kin see that curve o broon leg yit, sparklin wet, an fingurs strokin the airch o hur fit.

'Ye cannae say ah'm wrang,' ah shout.

He disnae answer. She luks it me, yin eebroo up, mockin. They walk oan ower the road an she's hirplin. Favourin hur richt fit. An ah'm bate, peened wi fury. There's a strip o white bandage showin, bund roon, inside hur shune.

Proposal

DOREEN WATSON

Aw goanie?

    Naw acanny

Wi kinyenno?

    Cos acanny

Wi?

    Cos

Aw goanie?

    Naw

Goan eh?

Migrants

Barbara Clarke

I won't be coming home
but I'm still there
in your blunt heart
a grey stone
threaded with a pink vein —
perhaps a saint
picked it up on the beach
reflected on his mission;

but he went home,
his mother probably
sat with a basin
cold like an outside privy

whipping up a pudding
her fat arms still soft and warm,
should they brush your
child face
peering over the edge of a
worm-eaten table.

I'll come back about the time
our father kisses your lips
in an ashen prayer
and I'll watch for the mouse
who comes quietly onto the hearth.

It's a good time of year
to pray for the light
walking over the yard
with our buckets filled
with fat black cherries
food for the saints
who are down by the mines
their fires more than
a celebration
more than a memorial

I'll not be coming home
to your soft knee
nor your blunt-fingered smile
but I'll remember
while I sit on the boat
making tea in a pan
and a party from a spoonful of jam.

Guatemala Soldier Boy

BARBARA CLARKE

I know when you hear him scream
as the whip in your hand
cuts his flesh
you are laughing and weeping
blood wetting your hand
tastes sweet mingled with sweat
you loose your grip
but go on hard whip his body
like an old-fashioned top
in a frenzy you are screaming
a child at the fair
your voice is his voice
which is cold and silent
his voice creeps through
your skin crawling up to
your mouth a spider touching
your lips as you lie asleep
and you wake screaming your insides out
you a child a boy giving your love
a wooden box filled with leaves
and she will take it to her parents
because soon your time to smell her
to lie with her close at night is
to come — but that same night
they made you a man

who now writes his name in blood
and thinks himself a butcher of pigs
fat pigs warm pigs with black eyes
you killed her and ten of her litter
all of them juicy and pink inside
squeals of pigs remember when you
hear the squeals of men they are pigs
whipping pigs hung up on hooks
they ripen you can taste the sweetness
sweat mingled with blood

Confession

BARBARA CLARKE

I lied
I told a man with a bushy beard
and eyes like snails
that I wrote everyday.
I passed the words like stones
which touched his lips
then turned to gold.
He swallowed, they trickled
down his throat like honey.
He waited with his small mouth open
a tiny hollow like a bird.
I smiled and supped at weak juice
in a cheap punch glass, the sort
with a seam still to be felt
a smoky amber glass.

I lied because in my mind
I get up at dawn to pray
and bathe in a warm fragrant place
drink tea from a fine blue cup
then sit at a desk
where words fall out of my pen
as easily as drops of blood
from a sliced finger, dripping and dripping
which nothing will stop save time

and looking up from the warm smooth desk
is a beautiful sky through a beautiful window
a bay of iris and daffodils
I am warm and not hungry.
In the evenings I light fires
and eat delicate cheeses
which taste sour, peel nectarines
which are sweet
lie down with songs and warm hands
stroking me.

I wanted to know he hadn't made it.
Catch the words, he coughed at me
like a bird in winter calling home its mate
to the tree of fingers
hanging limply over the pond.

The White Dog

SYLVIA PEARSON

BUSISIWE AND NOMVULA were walking barefoot over the cool grasses of a Johannesburg park, and circling the water-sprinklers as close as they dared.

'Ehg, Busi, now you have diamonds in your hair,' Nomvula giggled, pointing at the silver droplets spangling her friend's thick rug of hair.

'It will be the only diamonds which will decorate *my* body,' said Busisiwe, stretching her mouth ruefully as she collected the moisture from her head, and smoothed it with splayed fingers over her gleaming cheeks. 'When *will* the rains come, I wonder? This is the seventh year, and the mealies in the fields are becoming thin and dry. Only the *whites* can keep their grass green. *Our* soil is cracking and hard to work.'

'But a ring and a bracelet of elephant hair with some Swazi beads are just as good as diamonds, neh?' said Nomvula, ignoring the other's comments about drought. 'And I saw Lazarus Ndaba buy such things from Poori's shop only yesterday. Did he not give them to you this morning on the bus? I think he has the eye for you, Busi!'

'Ach, that Lazarus — I think he is a *moffie*: he sprays his hair and armpits with his sister's stuff. Ever since he started that job with Coca-Cola — in that red suit of his — he is like a *woman*! Even my boss said to him yesterday that he must come to the *front* door now because his smell is confusing the dogs!'

'This boss of yours — he has dogs, Busi?'

'Yah, he has five dogs — Dobermans — with jaws like a crocodile, and tails no longer than my finger, and pieces taken from their ears to make them look more ferocious.'

'Yech! How can you be in such a place with all those dogs, Busi? Truly, some of those whites care more for their animals than they do for their children!'

'Yah, but I never see those Dobermans. They are kept in a yard where I never go, but speaking of dogs, Nomvula, I will tell you something — but you must promise to tell no one in the township. Swear it!'

'I swear it, Busi. I will be as silent as a dead cricket!'

'Well, do you know Salome who works for the rich Jewish meddam in 107, with the big blue car which Henry Mtebi drives?'

'Yah, I know her.'

'Well, two days ago that meddam had a whole houseful of whites for the weekend (Salome says her meddam is mad for that game of bridge, and she asked a cousin from Pietermaritzburg who is married to a *Boerra*. Unfortunately he had to come too because his wife cannot drive.) *She* had hair like the brass candlesticks Salome showed me on her meddam's table; and her nails were like the bloodied claws of a feasting lion. And her smell, Nomvula, was like a thousand Frangipani flowers — yech! With them was a dog, white-white like the butterflies that once a year cover a part of the Karoo desert and then die. This dog was all the time smiling with very black lips. Its fur was deep up to a child's elbow. Salome did not like this smiling dog. You understand — she did not know its ways.'

'Yah, I understand Busi. Of course, she would not know its ways if it did not live with her meddam!'

'And you know how things are with Salome, and how long she has waited.'

'Yah, and how many tens of rands she has given to that sangoma for the throwing of the bones, and the infusions and oils!'

'And Salome is a sober woman now. Not one drop of liquor has passed her lips since her meddam took her from the streets of Sophiatown.'

'Yah, tea only — and coca-cola when Lazarus delivers to 107. Yah, truly, Salome is dry-dry — like our gardens.'

Nomvula giggled behind her hands, but stopped abruptly when she saw Busisiwe's frown. She coaxed her friend to proceed with the story. Busi wiped the sweat from her hairline with a finger, and folded her arms across her breasts. The two young women were nearing their bus stop, so Busi lowered her voice.

'In the afternoon of the Sunday when the 107 meddam takes her cat-nap this Boerra man ordered Salome to give his dog all that remained of the meal on the table, and you must know that there was much food because of the *big* eyes and the *small* bellies of those whites!'

Nomvula stared in horror, for everyone knew that maids like Salome who shared the same roof as their meddams, and could not cook mealie-pap and gravy, or chicken wings and red pepper sauce, depended on leftovers.

Busi nodded grimly. 'Yah, Nomvula, you have guessed it. Salome had to give to the dog with the smiling lips the veal and fish balls and squash fritters and potatoes and rice and spinach. *All of it!* The Boerra made her wait until the dog had cleared the mountain of food with its pink tongue and black lips, and then he ordered her to bring water for the dog.'

The two women exchanged grimaces of disgust, and Nomvula said, 'It is a pity that the meddam of 107 was resting or she would not have allowed this thing to happen.'

'You are right, my friend, and Salome was hungry for the

rest of the day with only some pieces of bread from her apron pocket.'

'That was not good for Salome to be hungry, Busi, especially at this time. It is a bad story, truly it is.'

'It is not the end of it yet,' said Busi, mysteriously. 'The Boerra did not take his smiling dog away from the 107 garden to do its *business*. In a few hours it emptied its bowels on the top step of the verandah leading down to the yard where Salome hangs the washing. Its mess was *green* and running from the spinach. The smell was very bad, and brought the dung flies. Salome was already feeling the sickness of her time, and she was also hungry. The Boerra was red in the face from whisky, and he was ashamed that the meddam should find his dog so bad, and that *he* was the guilty one, so he ordered Salome to clean up the mess quick-quick!'

Nomvula's hands flew to her face, and she gasped with revulsion. 'And did she clean the mess, Busi?'

'Neh, she did not clean it. How could she, with the way she was?'

'And what did the Boerra say?'

'He shouted at her to do this horrible thing, and threatened to beat her, but Salome would not look at him, and would not speak. He called her terrible names, but still she would not. And then he went into the house, and took a heavy knobkerrie from the wall. He beat her, Nomvula, on her head and shoulders, and even on her breasts which had just started to leak with the promise of milk. And then he asked her again to tell him why she would not clean up the mess when such a task should be part of her job.'

'Did she speak, Busi, did she tell him?'

'Neh, she did not tell him. She said only, "I cannot, boss, I cannot do this thing", and when she started to bleed from the blows, she ran up to her meddam's bedroom, and told her. The meddam came down, and took the Boerra boss into the house. Salome heard her lashing him with her tongue, and then she brought him to Salome in the small kitchen where the vegetables are prepared. The meddam was very angry, and begged Salome to explain herself, so she did, but she would not look at the white man's face, only his shoes. She said, "I cannot clean up your dog's mess, boss, because I am pregnant, and I am Zulu. To do such a thing would mean that I shall lose the child of my womb."'

'What did the Boerra pig have to say to that, Busi?'

'He was very, very angry, and stamped around shouting about us blacks with our "blerry stupid superstitions", but the meddam told him to be quiet, and that there would be no meal for him that night because Salome would be put to her room to rest, and that if her girl should lose the child — *he* would never come under her roof again — evah!'

'So, what happened to Salome?'

'Well, she miscarried, of course, from the beating, and now she lies in the Baragwanath hospital with the meddam from 107 visiting her every day because the husband cannot when he is in the Kruger gold mine.'

'Blerry dogs, Busi, they are a curse!'

'Egh, but listen to what happened to the smiling dog, Nomvula. The garden boy, Joseph, he had to clean up the mess. When Lazarus came with the coca-cola lorry they got to talking. You know that Joseph, neh? He used to be a *tsotsi*, but the meddam tamed him down so he no longer runs with the street gangs. Well, this Joseph asked Lazarus for some of the broken bottles from the box at the back of the lorry. He put the glass in a mealie sack, and hammered it down into small small pieces the size of diamonds, and mixed it in with some chopped livers and dog biscuit.'

'Ayee, ayee!' screeched Nomvula, covering her mouth with cupped hands.

'So now, Nomvula, the smiling dog is still smiling, but its lips are *red*, and it no longer breathes!'

'So, Busi, there is truly *something* to be said for *moffies* and *tsotsies* after all, neh?'

'Yah, my friend, there is something, there is — and for the meddam of 107!'

Blue Room in Greece

ALISON REID

This is a blue room in Greece
(Blue they explain is the colour of heaven)
In the corner the afternoon light
Is caressing the legs of a chair.

Over there in the opposite corner
clothes slump
Their insides have been taken out
And are just at this moment
Walking into town.

The town itself is perfect people
Eloquently tanned and debonair
I myself have washed my hair
And attempting to break into
an avocado pear with my teeth
have failed to affect
my surroundings.

Later in a grey room in Glasgow
(Grey I can see is the colour of rain)
In the corner the afternoon light
Falls asleep in the arms of my chair.

The Automatic Sensualist

Fiona Wilson

He's perfected all the rituals,
that cool-eyed boy.
Already his mind is programmed
to sensual over-drive and
love is on automatic pilot.
When he talks, it's as if
the ordinary words he chooses
caress the space between us.
He understands the catacombs,
the secret patterns of female speech.
Mistakenly we allow ourselves
to confide in him.

Winged Boat

Fiona Wilson

Close to sunset we found her floating
alone as a cut flower on a lake,
Marie Celeste, named at birth for this death.
True the light was dim, receding from the sky,
and land a distant and still cloud for us,
yet it seemed she rose above the waves,
half in water, half in air,
neither element sufficient for the perfection
of her absolute solitude. Empty boat,
hollowed of voices, the terrible, sensual grating
of many lives lived together. Washed away
to clean bone boards and planks creaking
like taut, wet ropes.
And nothing but us, and it, and sea,
and three black cormorants perched on the prow,
three rough charcoal marks burnt
against the opalescent heavens.

Briar Rose Dreams

FIONA WILSON

Suddenly it's all gone too far.
You're waking up alone
in the rose-scarred tower
knowing only that this is not
what you were led to expect.
While you slept the world was changed.
Now all the shutters are flapping
and no one is getting up
to close them. And somehow you can tell,
without even naming the thought, that outside,
your life story, the one they pinned on you at birth
is walking off, taking its swordtricks
and harlequin gee-gaws, past the granite fountain
and the frozen, moonlit waters,
past the winter flowering jasmine
that bloomed for a week, then faded.
You try to rise, to call a name.
You think that any name would do.
But you can't move, can't speak.
Because you were thinking, not speaking,
your body has become a nail pinning you
butterflyed, to the terrible, bland-faced bed.
And this is certainly not
what you were led to expect.

the sea is an anti-policeman

MAGGIE CHRISTIE

the sea
releases me
to repeat to repeat to repeat   the sea
un-accuses me
reassuring me
i am not boring   the sea
i may   go on and on   the sea
believes in me
supports me   upholds me   caresses me
mile after mile the sea
knows no orders knows no guns the sea
becalming endlessly

the sea   and i   breathe   the sea
endless   i breathe
endless   still   endless   moving   the sea

the sea
releases me
to repeat to repeat to repeat
i repeat
the sea
has an edge.   just one.   it is enough.
i land.

Untitled

MAGGIE CHRISTIE

Sweet sound, sea sound, music sound, silence
Sweet sea, sound sound, sound music, stop.
Sound sea, sound music, sweet sound, silence
Sweet silence, sweet music, silent sea, sadness.

The thought of you startles me like a poppy
An explosion of blood-red light

Sweet sweet sound, understanding of music,
Sympathy, carefulness, caring, sweetness.

Invisibility. Behind the breath control
The speech control. Support is necessary
To make the sound. Then real playing
Can begin. Unsupported breath
Makes expressionless noise, signifying nothing.

Unsupported love in my thoughts
And all around me too unseen.

Supported love is on display
The black cloud carries the sun away
Over the threshold to the wedding day.

Sweet sound, sea sound, music sound, silence
Sweet sea, sound sound, sound music, stop.
Sound sea, sound music, sweet sound, silence
Sweet silence, sweet music, silent sea, sadness.

You are a disruptive passage in a minor key
With jerky unanswered rhythms
The thematic connection revealed
Only on repeated hearings

Sadness.   Sea.   Silence.   Music.   Sweetness.

First Love

Susan Chaney

MARGOT ROSE TREMAIN was my first love. For a long time I loved her as passionately as I loved God, in fact I loved her more because Margot Rose, unlike The Almighty was a strictly forbidden pleasure.

'Your not to play with that girl,' said my mother. 'She's common. She lives on the council estate and she speaks so badly, I wouldn't want you picking up that awful accent. Her mother's no better than she should be.'

'I think her mother is very nice,' I replied. 'I think she looks lovely with her suntan and her gold earrings. I think she looks sort of foreign and mysterious like a gipsy.'

'It's ridiculous for a woman her age to dress the way she does. She has terrible varicose veins and she doesn't seem to care who sees them. She should spend less time sunning herself on the beach and more at home looking after her family. It's really quite disgraceful the way she lets those girls run wild with those awful names she gives them, they're bound to get into trouble. I shouldn't be surprised if they were all pregnant before they were sixteen.'

I thought the Tremain girls all had beautiful names, there was Margot Rose, Lucinda, Loveday and Camelia. They were all infinitely preferable to my own which was Hilary. Hilary! It sounded so dull and plodding like marmite and semolina pudding, brown bread and everything else that was good for me. It seemed to me to be the epitome of all that was hateful in my life, of all that was sensible and respectable and suffocating. It evoked Peter Pan collars, smocked dresses and Start-rite shoes, brown hair ribbons, liberty bodices and the necessity of eating up all one's greens.

'I bet Margot Rose never has to eat cabbage and spinach,' I would mutter rebelliously.

'I don't think that child has ever had a decent meal in her life. I expect they eat baked beans and chips all the time in that house.'

'Sounds alright to me.'

'That's enough, Hilary,' my father would say, lowering his paper and folding it meticulously, always a sign that he was about to make a speech. It was curious, but my parents, who were often and so bitterly divided were presenting a united front in their opposition to my friendship with Margot Rose.

'I don't really think that she is a suitable friend for you,' he continued, 'her father hasn't done a day's work in his life. He claims that he can't because he was wounded in the War. I never heard such nonsense in my life, the man seems perfectly fit to me, especially when he's playing football with his mates and drinking in the pub. It's an insult to the memory of all those brave young men who died.'

My father had lost many of his friends in the War and when he spoke of them his brown eyes looked so raw and helpless that it made me want to cry. He would sometimes speak of boyhood chums with names like Tiger Riley, Biff Baxter and Shortie Grub. It seemed impossible to me that anyone with names like these could have been blown to pieces in the desert or bayoneted by the Japanese in Singapore. They were boy's names, they spoke of midnight feasts, jaunts along the river and schoolboy pranks. They sounded eternally youthful, full of energy and an innocent zest for life. I couldn't believe that they had been wiped out in an instant, knowing only a moment of red, shrieking pain and then oblivion, forever. Neither could my father.

'Damn my eyesight,' he would often say. 'If only I hadn't been as blind as a bat, I would have been able to join the combat troops and fight with them instead of being attached to the Pay Corps.'

My parents, though well meaning, were not astute and they failed to realise that the more they counselled me against Margot Rose, the more determined I became to be with her.

On Thursday afternoons my mother drove into town to do her shopping and I had the house to myself. I would smuggle Margot Rose upstairs and into my parents' bedroom. This was forbidden territory and the enormity of the crime I was committing made me hot and nervous for hours beforehand. It was a large room, facing the sea, and it caught the sun in the afternoons. In the summer there was a clammy undercurrent of stale air which smelt of musty cupboards and heavy winter garments stored away in polythene bags. Thrusting through this came the sharper, more astringent scents of my mother's orange skin food, children's sweaty bodies and hot fabric. My mother was very houseproud and always drew the curtains before she went out to protect the furniture and prevent the carpet from fading. The warm, diluted light, pouring through the thin chintz curtains gave the room an added air of mystery, heightening the feeling of conspiracy between us. We crept across the polished, wooden floorboards clutching each other closely and starting with feigned drama at every creak or unexpected noise.

I thought Margot Rose even more beautiful when she was inside my mother and father's room as though the role of intruder suited her. Stray glimmers of sunlight from the window caught the gold tints in her tangle of auburn hair

and the pale light made her creamy skin look faintly luminous. Margot Rose hardly ever had to wear hair ribbons and
when she did they were never brown or navy but bright pink
or blue and printed all over with little silver stars. How I
longed to have hair ribbons like that! She never wore sensible shoes either but white toeless plastic sandals. 'Cheap
and Nasty' my mother said, but I adored and coveted them.

All in all I was her willing slave and well she knew it. We
would dress up in my mother's nightdresses and petticoats,
making veils and headdresses, fastening them around our
heads with her stockings. We would transform ourselves
into Princesses and Fairy Queens. Margot Rose always
seemed to get the best parts.

'I'll be Snow White,' she said, 'and you can be The Seven
Dwarfs.'

How I loved those long, secret afternoons we spent
together and I hoarded the memories close inside me. Later,
alone in my bed I would bring them out and turn them over
in my mind, letting them trickle into awareness like a miser
running a string of jewels through his fingers. I cherished
every moment we spent together, I would shiver with pleasure as I remembered the cool, silky feel of my mother's
bedspread, the tingly sensation of Margot Rose's warm
breath on the back of my neck, and the salty smell of her
skin.

I showed her everything. Crouched together in the small
curtained recess between the dressing tables where my
mother kept her private papers, I would open the old,
cracked white leather handbag and bring out her letters and
photographs. Our sticky thighs were pressed tightly together and I was shameless in my need to be accepted. We
opened the letters my father had sent in the early days of
their marriage when he was posted overseas in the Army
and giggled over the gauche sentiments he expressed. Later

these would be incorporated into our games and ridiculed. With damp, eager hands we rummaged through the drawers and once I showed Margot Rose an unfamiliar package that had been troubling me for some time.

'Dr. White's Sanitary Towels. Comfortable and highly absorbent. Ideal for those difficult days in the month,' I read out slowly, hesitating over the long words. 'Do you know what these are for Margot Rose? And what does, for those difficult days of the month mean? How can one day be more difficult than any other? At least how would you know it was going to be difficult before it happened?'

'Oh, those things,' she answered. 'We call them Jam Rags. Our Lucinda has to use them now. She says she bleeds like a stuck pig. She says it happens to every girl as they get older.'

'Will it happen to me?'

'Course it will, silly, it happens to everyone. I just told you that.'

I bundled the package hastily back in the drawer and slammed it shut. I turned to her and grabbed her hand.

'Well, I don't want it to happen to me and you. I want us to stay the way we are for ever and ever!'

Sometimes when we tired of my parents' room we would go into my eldest sister's and continue our explorations there. Marlene was nine years older than me and she was a remote figure in my life. She was nearly seventeen and she seemed to spend most of her time gazing out of her window or locked inside her room with her friends. She sighed a great deal and used a lot of words like 'Heavenly' and 'Divine'. She pretended that she could speak Russian and she played the violin, very badly, in front of the mirror, dressed only in a black lace bra and pants.

Margot Rose clutched Marlene's bra against her skinny chest and pirouetted around the room. Her eyelids drooped heavily and her lips pouted. 'Heavenly, darling,' she murmured. 'Quite, quite Heavenly.' I tottered after her in Marlene's blue suede stiletto heels, scraping raucously on the violin and whispering in what I thought were deeply thrilling tones, 'But Darling, you are Simply Divine. You are just Too, Too Divine.'

On Saturday mornings I would tell my mother that I was going to take my dog, Sam, for a long walk and then I would meet Margot Rose in our secret place beneath the crab-apple tree. The crab-apple tree grew half way up the lane that separated our houses and it was a natural place for us to meet. It was strange countryside around the crab-apple tree, strange and slightly forbidding. Once when Margot Rose had been late I wandered away from the road and found myself in the little wood at the bottom of the garden owned by the man who came from London. There was very little light and the ground was covered with a dark green, foreign-looking plant, that had fleshy leaves and evil, purple-coloured flowers. I was sure it must be poisonous and my skin flinched away from it. There was an inexplicable smell of rusting metal which troubled me. I thought of hatchets and knives and other dangerous implements that might be lying half-buried in the dank soil. It was very quiet at first and then I heard the very faint sound of someone crying. I crept closer until I could see the house. The man from London was sitting on the doorstep, with his head in his hands, sobbing as if his heart would break. I could see the top of his bald head, which was red and flakey with sunburn, and the tears squeezing out between his fingers and dripping onto the hot stones where they sizzled and disappeared as if by magic. I was horrified and disgusted. It was bad enough when my mother cried, but a man! I had never seen a man crying before. An old man at that, and he was crying in broad daylight. It was horrible.

Tears were for the darkness, tears were for the young. When I heard Margot Rose calling me from the road I turned and ran, forcing my way through the undergrowth and I didn't stop until I burst out into the hot sunshine and into her arms.

'There now,' she said. 'Its alright, don't fret yourself over him, he won't hurt you. He's just taking on something awful 'cos his wife left him.'

'How do you know?'

'I heard my ma telling her next door, said she didn't blame the poor woman neither, said no self-respecting woman could put up with that miserable old bugger.'

'My mother always makes me leave the room when she's talking to her friends.'

Margot Rose looked at me with a worldly expression far beyond her years.

'Well, your mother, Hilary, your mother's a bit gormless, isn't she? At least that's what my ma says,' she added hurriedly.

One summer, under Margot Rose's instruction, I devoted most of my time teaching Sam to attack wellington boots. I had a particularly horrible pair of boots which my mother made me wear even when the grass was only slightly damp. They had been passed down to me by a whole succession of cousins and I hated them even more than the brown felt hat with bunches of bananas above the ears that I had to wear on Sundays. They were made of a dull, red rubber and around the top was a band of mouldy-looking artificial leopardskin fur. They were the kind of boots much loved by old ladies. Sam was an easy dog to train as he was quite young and it was possible to work him into a frenzy of excitement just by repeating the words 'Canst thou see thine enemies!' in a certain tone of voice. I would run ahead and Sam would chase after me grabbing the leopardskin between his teeth, growling and worrying at it, shaking his head from side to side as if he were a wolf bringing down a sheep.

One afternoon when I was out in the town with my father I saw an old lady walking ahead in an identical pair of boots. Sam was trotting happily beside me and I bent down and whispered in his ear. 'Sam, Sam. Canst thou see thine enemies!' There was a few minutes of wonderful confusion with much snarling from Sam and startled screams from the old lady before my father managed to extricate the hysterical dog from the melée.

'Damn and blast that stupid animal,' he said. 'I just can't think what's got into him lately.'

I felt a mixture of fear and curiosity at the thought of visiting Margot Rose's house. I could always tell what I felt about a house from the way it smelt. As soon as I opened the front door and stepped into the hall of a strange house I could tell whether I liked it or not. Some houses always smelt cold and empty no matter how warm the day and some were full of intimidating smells like boot polish and brasso. In others the smell of stale cooking and cold grease seemed to accumulate just inside the door. I liked to think that I could guess what the family were like from the way their house smelt; that I could tell if they were going to be friendly and relaxed or formal and stiffly polite. This house had a wonderful, intoxicating smell of beer and fried eggs, make-up and clothes steaming in front of the fire. Mrs Tremain was obviously a casual housekeeper and things that would have been hidden away in my house were prominently displayed in hers. Bras and knickers were draped across the backs of chairs and a large bottle of Radcliffe's Worm Syrup stood on the kitchen table. Best of all though was the television. I didn't know anyone else who had a television.

'How can your dad afford to buy a telly if he doesn't have

a job?' I asked Margot Rose.

'Well,' she answered, laughing. 'Fell off the back of a lorry, didn't it!'

At first I was shy of Mr Tremain, he seemed so big and meaty compared to my own father, but eventually I found the courage to speak to him. 'Were you really wounded in the war?' I asked. He gave me a long, knowing wink and slowly tapped the side of his nose.

'Well now, my little maid,' he said. 'That would be telling, wouldn't it? Ask no questions and you'll be told no lies.'

Before I met Margot Rose I had been a lonely child seeking consolation in God. I felt I had a special relationship with God because my house was built just below the church and I thought of Him as my next-door neighbour. When I was very young I believed that God lived in the church tower, behind the clock-face. I confused the power of God with the chiming of the clock. 'God is always watching you,' I was told in Sunday school and at night when I woke and it was so quiet that I could hear the hum and whirr of the machinery as the clock prepared to strike I thought that it was God talking to me. The clock would strike the quarters and the halfs, the three quarters and finally the hour and I believed that this was God charting my way through the night, telling me exactly where I was and how long it was till morning, telling me that I was safe, that He was there. I would turn over reassured and go happily back to sleep.

I treated God's garden, the churchyard, as an extension of my own. I would go in through the back gate into the old neglected part of the churchyard where the rusty, iron railings around the graves had collapsed and lay decomposing in great tangles of nettles and goosegrass. Some of the granite tombstones were leaning over at crazy angles, half hidden by the feathery blooms of the elder bushes. Most of the writing on the headstones was so worn that it was impossible to read it and I would clamber up close and trace the letters with my fingers in an effort to find out who was buried there. It was my secret place, and I never told anyone about it, not even Margot Rose. I was always searching for the sailors' graves: I had been told a story once about a shipwreck and I knew that many of the drowned sailors had been buried in the churchyard. Their bodies had never been claimed because no one had been able to find out who they were. 'The Church of St Piran with the graves of the unknown sailors,' I would chant to myself as I thrust my way through the brambles and Cow Parsley that grew thickly around the graves.

I never did find the sailors' graves but I did find the place where all the babies were buried; it was a remote part of the churchyard, very quiet and still. Here most of the tiny graves were well cared for with fresh flowers and beautiful chips of coloured stone and loving messages inscribed with gold. All of them except one, which lay over in the far corner beneath the wall, a tiny mound of forgotten earth. 'Why had the child's parents left the grave like this?' I wondered. I would spend hours there pondering the mystery and concocting wonderful tales of tragedy to account for it. Perhaps the parents themselves had died from broken hearts or perhaps the entire family had been struck down by some fatal disease. In the end I decided that they just found it too sad to come to visit their baby and so I thought that I would look after the grave for them. For months I kept a jam-jar full of wild flowers and visited the baby regularly. It was the only secret I ever kept from Margot Rose.

I showed her where the Mee Mees lived in the huge stone water tank in the farmyard. I taught her how to catch them and make them a new home in a jam-jar. I took her to my excavations in the dark little shrubbery behind the single-storey wooden house, where poor, mad Mrs McGuire lived. I showed her the curious opaque china bottles and pots I had dug up. 'Mrs McGuire's a witch,' I told her. 'She uses these to mix her potions and poisons in. After you've touched them you have to wash your hands five times with carbolic soap and count backwards from a hundred at the same time. It's the only way to break the spell. Mind now, it has to be carbolic soap or you'll die. I know she's killed a lot of people and she buries them out here; it's only a matter of time before I find the bodies.'

When the tide was right out I led her across the causeway of slippery rocks. I was more agile than she was and I leaped easily from rock to rock ahead of her. When she called to me for help I raced back feeling full of a new confidence; as I took her hand I felt strong and protective towards her. Eventually we reached the end of the causeway and as we peered down through the shifting colours of green and blue light-dazzled water, where the thick brown streamers of seaweed swirled lazily in the current, I showed her the wreckage of the fishing boat. I was proud to share my world with Margo Rose, but I never took her to the baby's grave.

As we grew older our relationship had been changing and our clandestine Thursday afternoons were no longer occupied by children's games. We sat in front of my mother's dressing table practising in earnest with her make up and experimenting with each other's hair. When we had transformed ourselves to our satisfaction we would take all our clothes off and explore each other's bodies with curious fingers. Sometimes we would lie down on the bed and practise snogging and French kissing, tickling and wriggling till our breath came in sharp, hoarse pants. When we bathed together, inching slowly forward into the icy water, our screams contained a new awareness of each other as our bodies responded to the sensation of the sea seeping into the legs of our bathing costumes.

I spent a great deal of time in trying to persuade her to join the church choir. I thought that if only I could have Margot Rose and God together under the same roof then my happiness would be complete. How beautiful she would look in the choir stalls with the light falling through the stained glass windows and haloing her copper-coloured hair. How perfect she would be in the dark purple cassock with the white ruffle setting off her eyes and her pale hand resting on the deeply polished rosewood pew.

'Please Margot Rose,' I begged her. 'Please will you join the choir? Oh, please, please say that you will.'

'Don't be daft. I'm tone deaf and I can't sing a note.'

'But that doesn't matter, I can't sing either. The Vicar doesn't mind whether you can sing or not, he just wants to get enough people to fill up the choir stalls, especially girls, he's very short of girls. He's got a lot of boys, though,' I added slyly knowing this would interest her.

In the end I did persuade Margot Rose to join the choir but it didn't turn out the way I had hoped it would. She refused to take it seriously and mimicked everyone in the choir and the tiny congregation. As we proceeded solemnly up the aisle with the asthmatic old organ wheezing out a hesitant tune, Margot Rose would be convulsed with laughter and her singing would grow progressively louder and more untuneful. 'Be quiet,' I would hiss, digging her hard in the ribs. 'And stop that awful giggling.' She had the most shrill and pervasive giggle that I had ever heard. During the silent prayers she was always peeping between her parted fingers and pulling faces at the verger. As we recited The Lord's Prayer I could hear her saying 'Our Father who farts in Heaven. Now it's Halloween and he must have ate some beans.' When the Vicar was delivering his sermon she would make loud farting noises just to make the boys laugh.

'Will you shut up,' I said. 'You're being so embarrassing.'

'And you're being so boring. You're being a real pain in the bum.'

One Sunday morning she failed to turn up at all and so did Christopher Curnow, though I didn't notice it at the time. After the service had finished I raced home for Sam and ran all the way to the crab-apple tree, hoping that she would be there waiting for me. As I came round the bend in the lane I saw them. Margot Rose was leaning up against the tree, our tree! And Christopher was bending over her.

'How could she! How could she!' I thought. 'And with Christopher Curnow of all people. Christopher Curnow with his awful pimples and clumsy hands.'

She had smoothed all her lovely hair up into something which she called a French Pleat and she was wearing a turquoise-blue shift dress. 'Tarty', my mother would have called it. The dress was sleeveless and her legs were bare. It was too early in the summer to dress like that and her flesh looked pinched and blue, sort of sad and flabby.

They hadn't seen me and I turned away and crouched down beside Sam. I hugged him to me and pressed his cold nose against my hot cheek. I held him like that for a long moment until he began to whine and struggle to get free. When I looked over to the crab-apple tree, Margot Rose and Christopher had gone.

'Come on, Sam,' I said. 'Let's go home.'

The Undertow

V.J. MCCALL

Small child on the stretching sand,
still unaware of the undertow,
steps knee-high like a hackney,
into the friendly waves.
Little ones curl on warm flesh,
and now stiff-legging those ones
that roll up to that's far enough waist
and push on leaving tingly thigh.

10 9 8 7 6 5 4 3 2 1 zero
white (but not Kotick) small child,
self-dared through the eye-shut salt,
feels friendly wave's strong arms
catch, hold, smother, twist, upend,
and weave tightly into the undertow
in a rolling seesaw, tangle sand.

And have you felt it — that save-my-soul
fear insidious as freezing fog,
an undertow of what-ifs,
in a rolling seesaw tangle, jingling
beneath the surface? Happy manic
undertow, it giggled gorillas on the drainpipe and
fingers in the dark, but we all know eye-shut
better now, don't we?

Some Days

V.J. McCall

Some days are numinous
in the clarity-quality
of light
today was such that I could
touch the outline of the distant
pentland
and the clouds were puffing
gently uncrowded
in the blueing hemisphere —
no flat earth thoughts when
the incongruous straight
line of boeings' trail
up and across illustrate
the curving globe in
sudden geometric twins,
like atlantic salmon —
cock and hen companionably
beautiful
up-streaming to a dismal climax.

Some days are numinous.
After banging my head against
dreich rain drizzle days,
I am sun shot alive, with quiet
bliss so-never-the-same as
before her dying.

Edinburgh in July Heat

V.J. McCall

Oh it is rushy in hot
days of rippled skirts
to have business in the
Royal Mile.

It is summer and jungle
street heat days
have set the lithe
and willowy breezing

in floating floral glides
and they seem not busy
yet purposeful and I envy
their poise and their

peace unhurried with legs
that slip delicately
in step and step offering
receding in one move.

And the leisured stump
on soggy espadrilles and laced
round with cameras like
a sterile lei.

There are others who
command disregard with the
power of sweat and trial.
Those whom the sun persecutes

the pale and the obese who
struggle with the plastic
in their hands sticky-sticky
talcum streaking from the armpits

and the old the smiling old
man reduced in his tweed
with his smile melting into
his laboured breathing.

He is little and slender
like a girl so that in
a youth together I would
have missed his worth

But in March down days and July
heat he smiles past my window
never hearing my applause. And
may I smile so in my shrinkage

but gliding breezy-breezy.

Sundays

HONOR PATCHING

'Smash of the day!'
the announcer said
'Once more those old Home Service
comedies we all loved.'
But with those oh-so-jolly tunes
That signatured The Navy Lark,
Beyond Our Ken,
I am dyspeptic with my childhood,
with all the years of solid Sundays,
the viscous weight of Yorkshire Pud
and grey meat lapped by Bisto shallows
on a blue-ringed plate.

Back in that sunless kitchen
the electric fire sparks
and spits hot dust,
stuck in its hardboard fascia
that seals in the old hearth
and the ghost of the old black range.

Once my brother brought
a friend home who,
put next to me at table,
laid his hand upon my thigh
beneath the cloth and winked.

I sang 'Dream Baby' all
that weekend, thinking of escape
and adulthood. But when it came,
escape was just a painted fascia,
rickety and meretricious,
covering the old iron ghosts.

Tea on the Table

CHRISTINE QUARRELL

Patriarchal tea
steak for him
egg for me

The Whistling Postman

CATHERINE MACPHAIL

'HELLO LASSIES, and how are you the day?'

My sister, Ella, stopped clawing at my face and put on her sweetest smile. I hoped Tam, the postman, could see it for what it really was. A mask, hiding a vicious soul. I, however, smiled too.

'That's the ticket,' he said, slipping an arm round each of our shoulders. 'You canna be fightin' on a grand day like this.'

It was a grand day too. The May sun was shining in through the window on the landing and the whitewash on the close wall and stairs gleamed.

'I wasn't fighting with her, Tam,' Ella said. She was thirteen and up in the big school and felt she was much too much of a lady now to fight. 'It was her! She's a tomboy and a right wee scunner.'

Tam ruffled my hair. 'Here, is that right, Rose? are your a right wee scunner?'

'Well, I'm a tomboy anyway,' I told him proudly. Who wanted ever to be a lady? Who wanted ever to grow up? Not when so many exciting things could happen to you when you weren't. 'I've been picked to run for the school in the interschool sports.'

I'd been telling everyone since I found out, so chuffed to be picked. Me. Rose Mary Morgan.

'A good runner, are ye?'

'The best in the school.'

Ella tutted, but I said it without any vanity because I was. Even Rena Dunbar had to admit that. She'd never beaten me yet, though she swore one day she would. And she hated me for it, but not half as much as I detested her.

'Good for you, wee yin,' Tam said.

He would have continued down the stairs with us, but Mrs. Aitken on the first floor opened her door to ask him if there were any letters from her son in Canada.

'Mrs. Aitken,' Tam assured her softly. 'When I see a Canadian stamp on your letters you're the first one I deliver to.'

'Ach, Tam,' Mrs. Aitken's watery blue eyes overflowed. 'You're a right gem.'

He was too. Everyone liked Tam. His whistling as he entered the close filled it with more than music. The silence when he was gone made it seem emptier than ever.

He brought with him all the latest gossip from the other closes on his rounds, 'Wee Jack at 23 was lifted last night. Drunk again. Aye.'

He brought messages. 'Annie says you're to pop round after you've finished in the washhouse for a wee cuppa.'

Sometimes he even brought letters.

He had only been on our round for a couple of months, but already he had made his mark ... or his stamp, as I pointed out rather wittily, I thought, to my mother. She had laughed, and Ella had tutted and called me a wee scunner again. Her vocabulary is very limited.

That morning, even Ella couldn't spoil my mood, and meeting Tam only made me feel better.

I hurried, skipped, ran along the road to school after I left my sister. I would have to get into training I decided. The Intersports was only three weeks away, and I had to win. I hadn't been picked for anything before in my life. I wasn't clever, like Ella. I wasn't even as pretty as she was.

Hair like rat's tails, she would often tell me — and that was her being kind. My lips were too thick, my nose was like a dod of putty someone had stuck onto my face. Not that it ever bothered me. I didn't want to be pretty anyway. I wished I'd been born a boy. To make up for that mistake of nature, I almost was. I could run faster than any of them. I could fight better. And as my sister and Rena Dunbar often pointed out, I was built like one. Skinny and flat-chested …

Sister Mary Francis, our headmistress, hadn't wanted to choose me to represent the school. She wanted Rena Dunbar. But that was only because her mother was always sending up presents. It was Miss Telford, my teacher, who persuaded her I must be chosen. I sat outside the office and heard everything. 'Rose Mary Morgan will run her heart out for this school, Sister, I give you my word on that.'

There was no way I was going to let Miss Telford down.

Rena Dunbar was waiting for me at the school gates when I arrived. She was surrounded, as usual, by her gang of insipid friends. 'See you Morgan. You're goin' to be sorry.'

If she was trying to frighten me, she had chosen the wrong day. I was in no mood even to get mad at her. Instead I laughed.

Poor Rena didn't know where to look. If I'd slapped her face she wouldn't have been so affronted.

'Did you see that?' She looked around, her mouth hanging open. Her friends followed her cue, and their jaws dropped six inches. 'Do you think Ah'm kiddin?'

'No. I just think you're daft.'

'I'll show you who's daft!' She was on me in a flash, scratching my face, pulling at my hair. But that's another thing Rena can't do as well as me. Fight. In seconds I'd gained the upper hand and was sitting astride her, ready to pound a fist into her chin.

'Rose Mary Morgan!'

Miss Telford's voice screaming at me made me turn. It was all the diversion Rena needed to land her own punch.

Two Miss Telfords lifted me from Rena, both of them mad. It took a moment for them to merge into one disappointed face.

'Rose Mary Morgan, are you ever going to grow up? You're eleven years old. It's time you were behaving like a young lady. Fighting like a hooligan. Really!'

'But, Miss. She started it …'

'I don't care who started it,' her voice became softer. 'Look Rose, behave yourself. The races are in three weeks. I don't want Sister to have any reason to replace you.' Now, she smiled. 'I've put myself on the line for you.'

On the line … it was like something from a Hollywood picture. She'd put herself on the line for me. I would never let her down. Never.

That night I began my training in earnest.

After my tea, I ran round the block so many times, the neighbours sitting outside their closes in the warm evening grew dizzy watching me. Next morning, too, as soon as I woke up, I was off again, bringing in hot rolls for the breakfast on the way back. Actually, that was the only reason I was allowed out so early.

'Light mornin's or nae light mornin's,' my mammy said. 'You're no runnin' aboot the empty streets in a pair o' shorts.'

This, even though my dear sister assured her I'd be in no danger. 'Who'd look twice at a stick wi' a pair of legs?'

'Listen, there are some dirty ow' men don't care what you look like!'

I was in no danger … at least of getting big-headed about my looks.

'I'll tell ye something else,' Ella went on. 'She's no keepin' me late for school. I'm goin' away without her.'

Mammy had put her foot down about that, 'You'll walk up the road with your sister … and that's all about it.'

Every day I felt fitter and ran faster. I even thought about sending away for a Charles Atlas set — did they do them for girls, I wondered? They certainly worked a treat for Geordie. Although I didn't want to be muscle-bound. I wasn't that much of a tomboy.

And every day we would meet Tam as we came out of the house and he'd say, 'Not long to go now, hen? How's the training going?'

He'd insist on me flexing my muscles so that he could test them with his fingers. 'Would ye credit the size of that.' And he'd whistle so loud it almost hurt my ears.

Sister still walked past me, nose in the air, fingering the rosary beads that hung from her waist. Praying for something awful to happen to me probably so her beloved Rena could take my place. Her Rena was doing her best to help her prayers along. She baited me regularly, waiting by the corner with her friends, taunting me, wanting to get me into trouble.

I had friends too. The whole school was my friend, sure without doubt that I would win and bring them glory. I would win too.

I did my best to ignore Rena … except once, the day before the races. I saw her tense as I drew closer to her, expecting me to fight at last. I didn't. I only said in the most menacing voice I could muster, 'See after I win the morra. You better watch out. Because I won't care who I get into trouble.

My mammy was angry when I went out for my usual training run next morning. 'You're goin' to be all puffed out for the races.' She was excited too, and proud. She'd told all her friends about me. She'd even put up a candle to ensure my victory.

'No, I won't mammy. Honest.'

She insisted, however, I have a leisurely breakfast before leaving. 'If you're five minutes late this morning ... they cannae complain.'

Ella wouldn't wait for me, and for once mammy let her go on without me.

Tam was late too that morning.

He was coming down the stairs, whistling, as my mammy opened the door. 'Well, here she is, Tam. This is her big day.'

'She'll dae ye proud. Will ye no', Rose?'

He slipped an arm round my shoulder and my mammy closed the door.

'Are ye excited?'

'Aye, but that'll only make me run the better.'

'That's the ticket.'

He pulled me in close to him and I really didn't like that but he was Tam and I didn't want to offend him.

'See you, hen. You're special. Do you know that?'

His hand had moved from my shoulder and was round my waist now and his face, when I looked up to answer him, was too close.

'Thanks Tam.' He was only trying to be nice. I'd hurt his feelings if I pulled away. But I wished suddenly that I was out of that close ... away from him.

He was still smiling. What lovely, white even teeth he had ...

All the better to ...

Now why did that come into my mind? I giggled, and yet I wasn't happy. I was sweating.

We were at the bottom. Sunlight was streaming in the close, traffic noisy outside, people passing on the street. I felt silly. Though his arm was still tight around my waist.

'I've got something for you,' he said. 'To mind you of the day.'

He stopped by the door leading down to the cellars.

'Something … for me?' Now, that was kind. He made me feel guilty.

'Come doon her and I'll give it you.'

He opened the door to the cellars and I looked into his smiling eyes.

'Can ye no give it to me here?'

'Och, come on. Do ye want your wee present, or do ye no?'

So I went inside and he closed the door behind him and everything went black.

I didn't run that day. I couldn't. Nor could I tell Miss Telford why. Nerves, they put it down to.

'Who'll believe you,' he said. 'Everybody likes Tam.'

Who'd believe me right enough? It must have been my own fault anyway. Hadn't he told me so?

Miss Telford cried in front of me. She really cried. 'I can't tell you how disappointed I am, Rose. I'll never trust you again.'

Sister didn't cry. She only looked at me as if she'd gladly kill me if she could. How I wished she would. I wanted to die.

I was booed by the school when I went in the next day. And that was the ones who would talk to me. Most of them didn't. I had let everybody down.

'I've never had such a red face!' my mammy said. 'Telling everybody you were going to win a medal for the school. Why in heaven's name didn't ye even run?'

I wanted to tell her, so desperately. But what if she blamed me too? What if she hated me?

So I said nothing. Not even to Ella. Especially not to Ella.

I kept close to her though. On the mornings when we'd come out of the door and Tam would come whistling down the stair. I held on to her tight. I knew I had to keep her safe. I could never let her be alone on the stairs, even on a bright sunlit morning with the birds singing on the trees in the back green.

He acted as if everything were the same. But he never quite met my eyes and he never dared to put his hand near my shoulder again.

Worst of all was facing Rena Dunbar. I hated her I was sure even more than I hated Tam.

'Thought you were going to get *ME*, Morgan?' She laughed as I passed her, and I couldn't even look her in the face. She followed, taunting me, showing me up in front of the whole school. 'You're useless, that's what you are. See you, naebody likes you. You're dirt.'

And how could I argue with that? She was right. I was dirt.

She could shame me, humiliate me, she could push and jostle me. And I would never fight back. Not with a word, not with a look.

Rena had won. She was better than me and I hated her for it. I took all my venom out on her. In my dreams she died each night from one form of unimaginable torture or another.

'You'll have to snap out of this, lassie,' my mammy said often. 'I've never seen such a carry on just because you didn't run in a race.'

And I'd listen at the door, dreading the sound of his whistling as he came into the close.

Then one day it didn't come. Nor the next, nor the next.

'See Tam's been transferred to another round? Everybody's gonny miss him.'

My mammy cocked her head when she saw me smiling.

'I don't know what you're looking so happy for?' Then she ruffled my hair. 'Though it's nice to see that smile again.'

I began to live. Determined to forget. I'd show Miss Telford she could trust me. I'd show them all. No one was going to beat me again. Now *HE* was gone.

Before I could start, I knew I had to face up to Rena Dunbar. If I could show that I wasn't afraid of her it would all come back, everything I'd lost. Rena was my enemy. Revenge against her would be the sweetest.

I left the house early one morning to make my way to her street on the far side of the school.

There, I waited on the corner, ready to challenge her before school began.

She wasn't alone when she came out of the close. One of her friends was with her, and someone else. In between them, his arms draped around their shoulders, was Tam.

I stood back, so they couldn't see me and I watched. They were laughing — fair taken with something he had said. I saw his hand, his big strong hand, move on her blazer.

Here was my revenge. I didn't have to do anything. She wouldn't always have a friend with her. One morning, she'd be alone in the close, with Tam.

I imagined his hands on her, his big powerful, groping hands. I saw her face, crying, pleading.

See how she'd like it! See if she could win a race!

She was struggling, afraid, trying to push him from her … and suddenly, her face became mine, crying, pleading.

And I knew I didn't hate her that much.

I couldn't hate anyone that much.

I was sitting by the fire when my mammy came in with the messages. 'Are ye no at school? Whit's wrong?'

I turned to look at her wondering why I hadn't told her before.

'Mammy,' I said. 'If I told you I did something really

horrible. Would you hate me, mammy?'

Her eyes softened. She dropped her bag on the floor. 'You could never dae anything really horrible, hen.' And she came to me and laid a gentle hand upon my head. 'Tell your mammy all about it.'

And for the first time since it happened, I cried.

Songs in Winter

Barbara Clarke

We carried water in old paint cans
the damp earth clogging our shoes
fingers burnt by the cold
I stood awhile in the kitchen
on clay flagstones decorated with shells
crushed in a bucket of blue veined stone

my stomach aching with a new heart beat
already crying with the cold
my soul had long since darkened

I left blood on your lips from kissing
in your arms you carried holly
with berries like adolescent nipples

in the dark we lit candles — magic light
old fruit wine would make me beautiful
and I'd sing you a song

it was a hard time, all those evenings
when you scraped back your chair
and said I'll be away then,
I'd nod and say you'll be away then,
eyes searching the floor in the dim light
for buttons pulled off in a panic
earlier in the day you shouting and spilling

the water from cans so its coldness bit my toes —
then making me stand naked to dry in front of the fire

in your bed tonight
I'll put a pouch of purple silk
and ten fish bones
your sleep will be of torment

it's that time of the year when breath
is like a deep knife cut
smarting as the air binds flesh to flesh
but I have some songs
I keep locked in a box
an old man gave to me

and when you've gone
do I sing those songs
alone with my fire
alone with my fire.

Mallards

BARBARA CLARKE

My voice torn away
like a mask
I hold it in both hands
deliver it in a porcelain bowl
with cinnamon and daisy stems

on the brow of the shed hang
six mallards
the evening making emerald of their necks

where do the pelts go?
if I had a voice I would ask for a quilt
to be sewn with the new skins of the mallard

I watch for two weeks the mallards shrivelling
swelling with worms

at lunch a woman with fat arms holds up a
wishbone
it cracks
my mouth pushed up to the window
cold and wet
finds a voice
the shrill lonely cry
of mallards flying nightward
over the lake

Winter Garden

BARBARA CLARKE

I went to see if the beach hedge had rusted
it was that time of year holding hands behind
the wall of red and rusting leaves
I saw a man take off his coat and lie down
his face came off in pieces but his lips
stayed blued to his mouth
out of his eyes came a raven
it hopped and stared back into the
liquid of eye like looking in a moonstone
on a wrinkled hand
the bird pecked pulling out the longest
and whitest of worms —
all the while the blue lips sang lullabyes
song stilled the air that soft soft stillness
of sunday mornings when the moon sits in
the piebald sky
I watched till his sleep was gone and his
mask put back on his face
and I knew I had come too early.

Being Intimate

Maureen Sangster

O when ye pit yer hand doon
tae the place it fits
it feels like gid sweet sherry works
bamboozlin tae the wits

I've rin oot frae ma human coat
I'm like a plant that slips
I'm slippin frae the tabletop
Ma pot'll drop! Ma pot'll drop!

I hae three breasts upon ma chest
Yer sweet head's one o them
Ye flung ma jumper far enough
but now ye're makin friends

I hae a flight o seagulls
that's liftin through ma head
O catch their wings, those lovely things
and tuck yer hands beneath
their soft white breasts

You curve ma back
I shape yer arm
We're sure of what we do
We're rapidly escapin frae
a box o a bedroom

The angles are a altered
The ceilin's bashin through
O knobble nibble knobble
knobble knobble nibble noo!

That window looks fair gackit
Has it got a new view too?
Instead o streets an city muck
does it look to frothy blue?

For I feel we are on holiday
nae in a city pit
so unrestrained
let's begin again
being intimate

Untitled

Maureen Sangster

somewhere nowhere
our baby is, is not
perpetual contradiction
always remembered

will always be seen
in our mind's eye
as he was on the ultrascan
superb TV personality

somewhere nowhere
something remains
what I did then
what I do now
what I have become

a stone angel sits
crying in a photo
I cut out from a paper
how, accurately, I chose
grief for a dead child

somewhere nowhere
pointlessness absence
total absence
people have children
we do not have

somewhere nowhere
is here this land
where children's minds
articulate what
we're not allowed to hear

three sons, three children
this father goes shopping
my world has not got
such swift particulars

we draw in our heads
the social contract, silence
something wrong subtracted
from us looms abstract

a lack child —
lessness a death
before there was
a formed enough child

somewhere nowhere
we know our place
our trackless
yet still resisting place

not only do we
insist on why
what happened did
we insist on why

this isolation a mist
a fog we whirl insist
don't you know of us?
we'll tell you

To Christ

MAUREEN SANGSTER

Oh Christ, ye're juist a meenister
ye're nae bloody eese tae me
ye winna come an mak
ma mither's tea

a stuck up little mannie
bawkin oot yer words o Love
for God's sake, come doon tae earth
an wear the oven glove

fit wye is this, Messiah,
that I maun lose ma life
carin for ma mither
fan ma brither's got — a wife?

if ye'd come roon on Sunday
gie me a helpin hand
one shot o handlin the commode
an you wid understand

ma life is juist a constant roon
o meals and bloody peels
if the hand o God is in this, Christ,
it's a mystery nae revealed

Single Parent Family, Ardnamurchan, 1837–54

JENNY ROBERTSON

[1.]

He came to me in June evenings,
when light lingers long.

I led my brown heifer by the shore, and sang.
Those sunlit days are gone.

'I am called Iain,' he said,
and the name shone like summer laughter.
'The chief's son,' I asked, 'from across the water?'
He smiled. 'The same.'
I promised never to repeat his name.
A ruin mo chridhe!

[2.]

My father, a godly man,
could not countenance the black disgrace.
'It's the parish for you now, lass.'
I said, 'The parish will suffice.'
My mother, keening, uttered one long moan.
I wept as I left my home.

[3.]

I am brought to bed with twins,
a boy and a girl —
they have your looks, my love.

The session clerk demands:
'Who fathered these twins?'
I say, 'I never knew his name.'
'No need,' replies the black coated man,
tight-lipped.
'You knew more than his name.'

[4.]

The boy is sickly. I sing a charm
to shield my babes from ill and harm.

Take upon you love of Mary mild
as she nursed her homeless child.

Take upon you strength of holy bride,
power of rock and storm and flooding tide.

Take upon you blessing of Colum-cille
to guard and keep you from hurt and ill.

[5.]

1839. The Poor's box disburses another pound for payment
of doctor's fees.

'Love is easy, love is light,
when summer's long and days are bright —
but there is a price to pay,'
the doctor muses, takes his fee.

'Will your lad not share your shame,
give his name, accept the blame?'
This learned doctor does not know
your touch brought larksong from the sky

your laughter lit shore and brae,
gave me wonder, gave me worth
gave me these twins I brought to birth.

[6.]

You are chief's son. I would not see you sit
three weeks upon the penitential stool.

I receive pence, barley meal,
darn, knit;
go out and gather cockles in my creel.

Watch my bairns grow, pinched, thin.
I whisper your name when I pray.

Water brought you to me.
I have heard that water carried you at length away.

[7.]

The news-sheet reports: In the Highlands they are preparing
in almost every quarter to go to America. Indeed, considering the extreme scarcity, even bordering on want, that
prevails in many districts, it is no wonder that emigrations
should take place.

[8.]

Water, says the spae-wife,
half a world wide, half a world long
sunders kindred, birth-ties, song.

[9.]

'Removal,' says the laird's man, 'is the only means
of ridding unprofitable land of feckless folk.'

'I am drawing up a list,' says he,
'of arrears, with names of those who cannot pay.'

'It were good,' he adds, 'to see
the remaining tenantry better lodged;
and I am under the impression ma'am, er, miss … '
He speaks the Southern tongue. Another man
interprets, reckons, writes.
' … that any payment you make
will be slight.
Therefore I am expecting you to emigrate … '

The man — I will not utter his traitor name
translates again.

I hear black words from his mouth:
'Australia … gold mines in the south,
opportunity, wealth.'

'Now there's the deal,' says the laird's man.
'In any case, no matter what you have to say,
I am sending you and your children away.
Good heavens, woman, would you have them starve?'

[10.]

I have lived here always
surrounded by wide skies and islands.

I twist grass to make baskets
and rope to tether,
with stones, our turf roof.

I know the good properties
of berries, wild flowers.

My language rinses my mouth
like water springing unsullied
amidst sunlit hillsides
fragrant with thyme.

Now all this is ended.
The laird's men put fire to our thatch.

Smoke stings my eyelids like tears.

My young ones are with me
and the taste of our anguish
is bitter, ah, bitter as hunger
salt as the sea.

Immoderate Conception

JENNY ROBERTSON

She sits unmoving, though the bairn inside,
restless, ripples her distended dress.
Dark eyes swim in her pale face.
Her hair is frizzed. The ends are split and dried.

Her mother, busy with necessities,
shops, saves coupons for a pram.
A few girlfriends, curious, still come.
She no longer fits their shape; embodies
their most secret fears, bulges
dread at what's ahead, yet finds her long wait hard.
'Three boys took it turn about out in the yard,'
the mother says. 'No proof of who the father is.

She never said a word; we've only just been told.'
The mother chainsmokes distress, stubs one word
against the next. The girl's thoughts are unheard:
fourteen, and heavy with thrice-fathered child.

Viking Brooch

JENNY ROBERTSON

Although the dead cannot hear
they buried her with the sound of the sea in her ear;

dressed her in kirtle and sark with skill and care,
fastened brooches she favoured for festive wear.

Silvered gold, slender pin, rich interlace
shone beneath her motionless face.

They brought her infant, dead at its birth;
shrouded mother and child with stone and earth.

Centuries unravelled clothing and flesh,
unstitched the bairn on the withered breast;

until a plough struck against the burial stone,
uncovered rare gold gleaming on a knotwork of bone.

Her jewellery was taken, classified, assessed,
ticketted, displayed behind casing and glass.

Her grave is hidden by thistle and grass,
where the sea's requiem enfolds her, and cloud shadows
pass.

Love Came Down

Franzeska G. Ewart

It all began one morning as I was on my way to get the potato scones for Jack's lunch. Jack likes a fried lunch on a Wednesday, you see, and to make sure that the potato scones are good and fresh, I always collect them from the baker's at ten o' clock. I've always taken pride in having things fresh — that and cleanliness, in the home, are so important I think. Not that Jack appreciates it, you understand. I'm sure he doesn't.

As I went down the front path, I happened to glance over the lawn, wondering, I think, whether it could do with another going-over before winter came in, when I saw this kind of burnt-out circle, right in the middle. At first I thought it must be those boys from the estate, always tormenting the cats and spray-painting the telephone booths, but when I looked closer I couldn't understand how they could have done it really. It was such a big circle, about six feet or more across, and it was the same thickness all the way round, as if it had been measured out somehow. Those young boys wouldn't know how to draw a circle anyway, so I went right close up and had a really good look. It was as if it had been poured over with acid or something, that had sort of made it shrivel and turn yellow.

I was just going to go back in and tell Jack to get some grass seed and I was wondering if you could plant grass in November, when I saw a thing that looked like a bulb, lying almost in the middle of the burnt circle. I thought it was one of the tulips Jack had planted just that week, but when I picked it up it wasn't a bit like one. It was a funny looking plant, and no mistake, but I was sure it *was* a plant, because it did have a flattened bit at one end and pointed bit at the other, and the pointed bit looked as if it was sprouting. There was a sort of shoot that had a greenish look, but it wasn't only greenish, it had red spots all over it. The outside was dry and crusty just like a bulb, and there were bits flaking off. I took it into the house and I told Jack about the lawn. You would have thought nothing had happened to see him.

It's a funny thing, but although I've been married to Jack for over thirty years, and we've reared and married off three children, just about at that time, at the time of the burnt circle, I'd been having funny kinds of feelings about him. I'd look at him sometimes as he sat at his paper and I'd wonder … I'd wonder things that I didn't have proper words for. It was more sort of … feelings. Like I'd think, was it always like this? And I'd have these kind of thoughts, when I'd wonder if there wasn't maybe … more. Yet I couldn't tell you what more was, and I didn't know why I was having the feelings.

Anyway, he said he'd look at the lawn when he had finished the crossword, and he said that he didn't suppose the circle would run away before then. And he promised to treat the lawn when he got the time, though heavens alone knows what else he has to do, apart from the football pools. And I went to the baker's for the potato scones, and on the way back I bought a little pot for the bulb, or whatever it was.

I planted it after I had done the dusting and hoovering. I know the modern thing is to take short cuts in the house-work, and there are a thousand labour-saving devices to let you, but I've never been one for that. I believe there's a right way and a wrong way, just like in life itself, and if you take the wrong way, sooner or later you'll be found out. So I clean the house from top to toe every Tuesday, Thursday and Saturday, and in between I just make sure it's dusted. That way I have plenty of time for the shopping and the cooking, and of course washing and ironing the clothes.

I planted it very carefully. The little pot I had bought for it was such a silly extravagance, so unnecessary. I didn't really understand then why I had bought it, when I could have used any of the dozens of brown plastic ones in the shed. It looked oriental, with orange dragons crawling over big blue flowers … a sort of garish pattern and not at all my taste. I pressed it gently into the potting compost, and as I did I felt the dark peaty soil on my fingers, and for a moment I had the same kind of feeling I had been getting when I looked at Jack. Daft, it was, but somehow I thought of all the things that had died to go into the soil, and what would grow out of it. I never thought about the soil before, I don't think.

Then I covered up the pot with a paper bag to keep the light out, and put it away in the cupboard under the stairs. Jack got grass seed the next week, and two weeks later he sprinkled it on the burnt circle.

I know that usually bulbs take months to come through and you just have to forget about them, but this thing poked a shoot through after a few weeks, a little red and green spotted thing. I took off the paper bag and I put the pot on the windowsill of my bedroom. Jack and I have had separate bedrooms for years, ever since Fiona left home and we had the space. I like it much better. I don't think I ever liked sharing a bedroom, even when we were young. I think it was because Jack snored. In any case, if you see one another all day every day, it's nice to get away during the night.

The first thing I did every morning when I got up was to

go across to the windowsill and look at the bulb. It grew a little every night, so I could always see a difference. As it grew taller, it widened out as well, and you could see it was covered all over with the red dots. They didn't look real, somehow. They were so exact, it looked as if someone had painted them on with red, shiny nail-varnish.

I started having the dreams around that time. At first it was just the odd night, then it was nearly every night. Hot dreams, they were, and there was a beating, a pounding in them. If you can dream a rhythm, then that's what they were. It was like being inside a great huge heart, or maybe lots of hearts all around. It was so hot and clammy, and there were smells I didn't know. I had never dreamt a smell, but every time I had this rhythm dream I woke up with this scent in my nose, as if it was in the room with me. It was like pepper, but sweet and sickly. Sometimes I used to think I could smell it during the day too.

And at the same time as I was having the dreams, the funny feelings with no words came more and more often. Whenever I saw Jack, even when I thought about him when he was in the garden, these feelings came. They began to form into words, though, almost on their own, and the words weren't like the kind of words I'd ever use, but like ones from a book or a television play. I'd be looking at him, and he'd look so fat and so old and so pink and wrinkled and slow, and I'd think, 'Slim, lithe bodies under tropical skies sway to the rhythms of my dreams.' I wouldn't actually see it, but I would feel and smell it, just like when I was asleep.

At first it scared me, because I couldn't understand it and I couldn't control it. I have always prided myself on my control, and I have always disliked uncontrolled behaviour in other people. It used to upset both Jack and myself when our Fiona started bringing her friends to the house. They were such strange young people she took up with. Always seemed to look half-awake and always talking about things which in my day were not discussed, and certainly not in mixed company. And no control at all. Often, I'd come into the front room and find a boy and girl (or what I took to be a boy and a girl, and I certainly hope they were for what they were doing) just stretched out on the settee and … well … with no thought to who might see them. Jack and I never carried on like that, even when we were married. There was always a time and a place.

When the plant was about six inches tall and had three wide leaves, something began to grow up from its middle, a long thin stalk, and there was a swelling on the end of it that got bigger as the stem grew taller. I got so excited about this because I knew it was going to be a flower. It grew much taller than the leaves, and they began to curl under, away from it, and yellow slightly as if they had done their duty and would soon die. The stalk was very stiff and strong, a reddish green that turned a deeper red further up so that the actual bud was dark pink. It reminded me of a garlic, because it had a lot of separate parts all held together by a pink outer skin. Sometimes I thought it looked rather evil.

When the flower started to appear, my dreams lasted the whole night, and they were so strong I found it harder and harder to wake up out of them. It was as if I went some-where else, not even just another country, but somewhere so different that the smells and the rhythms were more important than the words. And as I got more and more into this new place, the washing and the ironing and the hoover-ing were left undone and I was carried through each day on the crest of a gigantic wave of rhythm and scent. I would see Jack in the garden and as he turned to come in for his tea I would throw off my apron and I would hear myself say, 'Old man, come in for your tea but let me out, let me free of you.' And I would run out to the park, and walk under the trees and I saw the wintry sunlight cast through their leaves as I had never seen it before.

I just couldn't settle at all during that time when the flower was forming and ripening. I really felt like that myself, as though I was changing inside and was about to somehow burst out. It was a terrible time, in a way, but in another way it was very wonderful. Scary, but wonderful. Things seemed so new, and so ... alive, in ways I'd never noticed. I saw the colours of things as though they actually glowed. I would look at a perfectly ordinary thing, like the next-door cat sitting in the sunlight, and it would be all on fire and full of such beauty, that I would keep saying to myself things like, 'Why have I never before seen that that was so wonderful?'

Jack thought that I'd taken leave of my senses, he really did, and he spent a lot more time with his pals at the pub. He didn't like the house being a mess, you see, and meals appearing at any old time. I think he suddenly saw what he had lost, and he couldn't stand it. But I couldn't explain what I was feeling, not to anyone, but especially not to Jack. I was seeing all this beauty and wonder in all the ordinary things around me, but it seemed to make him look more ordinary. The brighter all the other colours became, the greyer, more invisible he got. I did not care at all about him. He could as easily have been dead.

It all came to a head in one night. I had been putting up the Christmas tree. Our Deirdre and her three were coming on Christmas day, and suddenly on Christmas Eve I wanted it to look so nice. I had more or less forgotten the season and all, and then I just woke up to it and I rushed to the shops and I bought new decorations for the tree and for the room, all sparkles and colour and light. I got things like angels that flew round lights that flashed, and a stable scene with figures that moved up to the crib when music played, and all kinds of other trash. I just loved it all. I must have spent a fortune.

I went to bed very late on Christmas Eve. I still didn't want to sleep, and I played my little radio very softly. It was Christmas music, 'Love Came Down at Christmas,' I remember. Then another noise began, and it slowly got louder until it drowned out the singing. It came from over by the windowsill, where the plant was. I didn't need to turn on the light to see that the flower was full out. The room was full of a bright light that seemed to come from that flower. I could never find the words to describe it. It was red, but no red was ever like it. It was like a red that had all the colours in it, and in the form of pure light. But it wasn't just colour, you see. The flower had so much more than just colour the way we see it. It had sound and it had such a scent … the peppery sweetness, and bitterness, and sharpness … it had all the scents of this life and the next. It *was* perfume. That's the only way I could say it. It was colour. It was sight. And it was sound. And I knew that there were, that there are, far more sounds and scents and sights than ever I can hear and smell and see. But that night I got close to the origin. I believe that night I saw God, and maybe it was important that it was Christmas, too. I just don't know.

You see, there was something more than all these things you can pick up with your senses, in the way we can pick things up. And I could only call it love, because I don't have any other word. Maybe it was a bit like Christ coming here, or at any rate, maybe it was the way those shepherds felt when they saw that baby. I don't think they took it all in either. I really don't think people can. I think it's too much for us.

And they came and took away the flower. And before they did, that flower had had all its seasons, and it was quite shrivelled up and finished, and I did not mind in the least that they took it, because really there was nothing much left to take. I had had the life of it. As they took it, I could see that it was covered with red seeds, quite big, hanging from little threads that had burst out in its lightning autumn. I do not know who they were, the owners of that plant, but I do not need to know. I only need to know that they came and they left me what I could understand, and they did not take away anything that wasn't theirs. I don't need to know any more than the shepherds needed to understand the movement of the stars.

When they were gone I slept, a sweet, cool, dreamless sleep. In the morning the snow covered the burnt circle I knew would be there. I thought that I'd wait until after Christmas before I broke it to Jack. I laughed, and felt such warmth when I thought of him, that I even thought I'd go out myself this time and buy turf and lay it myself come the spring.

So that is what happened, and now everything is back to normal and Jack is much happier and spends his evenings in. I clean the house from top to toe on Tuesday, Thursday and Saturday as I always did, and I go to the baker's to buy fresh potato scones on a Wednesday. To see me, you wouldn't think that anything had changed at all, and I never talk about the plant or anything that I saw.

But a lot has changed, you know. You can only tell from little things. Like the way I always sing when I'm hoovering. Or if you saw the way I sometimes polish the hall floor, with dusters tied to my shoes like a skater. And of course the change in the house would show you too, the plants that grow all over the place, in nice, bright, some-would-say-garish pots.

Tomorrow I'm going shopping again. I'm going to try

and find another two little pots with orange dragons climbing over big blue flowers. I'm going to fill them with rich dark peat, and into each one I'm going to press, ever so gently, a red seed.

Song of Sixpence

ANNE MACLEOD

Each Sunday she made apple pie
with neat fingers
plied the pastry quilt around
the fruit
      no serpent here, no tree,
apples cored and peeled, sliced, tossed
in caster sugar into the once-white enamel
tin, its blue edge wandering

she worked at speed
to sheath the frosted flesh before
the rot could
set pastry leaves feathering
the blackbird's open
beak
the beaten glaze
and neat fork-pricking

unhardened
she risked all in the snaking fire
each Sunday, with burnt fingers

Walberswick

for Charles Rennie Mackintosh

ANNE MACLEOD

In Walberswick the lilies danced
slow delicate life and you
delicately painted them
elegant, erect.
Fritillary — snakeshead lilies —
flowers you might well
have fashioned in a moment's
art nouveau experiment.
Life was not sweet, and yet the calm
elegance remains
order imposed on chaos, anarchy resigned
to the smooth curve of nature's architectural entropy.
In Walberswick the lilies danced
as if for you alone
slow delicate death.

Ornamental Onions

Olivia McMahon

Planted in late autumn they appeared
Just as we thought they'd gone
Underground.

Heading upwards, unbending stems,
Small globes forming in papery skins,
Slowly, cautiously, they unwrapped themselves
Thimble rough and green,
Mutinous.

We realise now they will not change
They carry their brightness within them
Not giving much away
Around them the extravagance
Of poppies and delphiniums.

Dear Fiona

Janette Walkinshaw

Dear Fiona,

Nice to get your letter and hear how the family are.

Glad you got the invitation but sorry you can't come. As you say, you will see the whole thing on television which is as good as being there. Everybody that is related was invited, and what a time we had, racking our brains in case we missed anyone and gave offence. George even remembered a second cousin of his that went queer and went to live in Paisley, and we put him on the list. I don't know if he opens letters but at least we tried. When I say queer I mean funny.

We've had a time too with the clothes. Jimmy says all the other women will be in black, and I wouldn't want to embarrass him on his big day, but black is just for old women, so I settled in the end for a kind of clerical grey lace which I thought was quite suitable. We had a rehearsal, just in the living room, of our part of the ceremonies and the train kept tripping me up so I've had to shorten it.

I've been practising going down the stairs backwards and everybody in the close comes out and pretends to be the cheering crowds, so as to get used to the real thing. The men don't have any choice about clothes, of course, it's top hat and tails again. George says if he'd known there would be all this palaver every time Jimmy got promoted he would just have bought the outfit in the first place instead of hiring it at great expense every time, but as I say it's not every day your son gets elected Pope so we shouldn't complain. Jimmy says it will be the last anyway.

Your Aunt Glenda says she's just wearing her ordinary clothes, and I am not very happy about this. She is in her Che Guevara phase just now, dresses like him, twenty years after everybody else, but that's your aunt Glenda, always at the cow's tail. My mother says it comes of being a late baby. But I can't help feeling it might cause some difficulties.

You ask how you should address Jimmy if you write to him. I don't know. It's quite a problem, isn't it? We've decided it would be daft for George to call Jimmy Papa, with Jimmy calling him Dad, so we will keep it informal in the family. And you should too. When I go up Byres Road my messages, people keep stopping me to offer congratulations, and I've a job explaining to some who are puzzled, with George and me being staunch Methodist, but as I say you can't tell the young ones nowadays. It's themselves for it. George blames himself for letting the boy go to the yooni, instead of a good technical college to learn engineering. He says Jimmy could be the Manager of Scotrail Provincial by now if he'd stuck in. However, it's all water under the bridge, or wine down the Tiber as Jimmy tells me they say in Rome. Only they don't say wine.

You would have laughed. With all this carry-on we've had a lot of people coming and going, security men, Heads of State, chancers, you name it we've had it. But I had a minister at the door the other day and he said he was here on behalf of the Godfather. I brought him in and gave him a cup of tea, and a good talking to. I said it was a disgrace him being mixed up with criminals like that and him a man of the cloth. But it turned out that he was looking for the Simpsons up the next close who have a baby due to be christened. I was that embarrassed, but the man took it all right. Jimmy says you shouldn't judge by appearances.

I'll need to finish this, Fiona, and get it posted. We fly from Abbotsinch first thing tomorrow and I've still got to pack. I don't know whether to put some woollies in or whether I will just need light things. I've asked Jimmy what the weather is in Rome, but you know what men are like. I couldn't get any sense out of him.

Love to the family,

Your aunt,

Maggie.

The Dark Coming

HELEN LAMB

On the back doorstep
waiting for the first star
and in the kitchen
ma chops up the onions.
The girl says — why don't we
just stand here together
and watch them all come out
until we lose count
we can watch the dark coming
but please don't cry.

Flotsam

HELEN LAMB

I am the fortunate flotsam.
Though I have no special grace
I weigh light
and so I glide
on the fluctuating waves.
Lack of substance is my strength.
It's a grave impediment
when drowning men cling on to me.
Not to mention the drag ...
... if you catch my drift.

Solitude

HELEN LAMB

He's a cold child
with a strange old face
and all he wants is
to be warmed
as he slides
his slight shivering form
between our skins.

So solitude lies down.

Wherever we go
he comes too
just slips in between
as if he belongs
and I want to ask
— did you bring him along
or did we create him between us?

Cave Woman Hand

Magi Gibson

As a child I played my games alone.
My closest friends were Water, Earth and Stone.

I loved to dip my hand into soft mud
then press it flat on cold grey stone.
I'd smile to see the mark I made —
five fingers a small palm held
bravely up to halt the march of Time.
But Time ignored my child's command —
she called her cohorts, Wind and Rain.
My handprint soon was gone.

Such games are now a thousand years away
At least it seemed that way until today.

Today I heard a guide explain
in France, deep underground
how a woman pressed her hand
against a chilly cavern wall
then on it blew soft ochre paint
through a hollowed reindeer horn
(just for the fun of it, that's all).

I wonder if she smiled to see
a slender wrist, a stencilled palm,
five fingers — fine, feminine, outlined

left behind
for twenty thousand years.

I can't begin to understand the distance spanned
by twenty thousand years.
Even on the abacus of stars we both have shared
I can't add up that far.

Yet still I recognise the game she played,
I smile to see the stencil shape she made:
her pre-historic human hand
her long ago cave woman hand
looks just the same as my hand does today.
Now childhood doesn't seem so far away.

Balance

MAGI GIBSON

At sixteen I was metal
you magnet — big attraction for
an iron maiden.
I never meddled in mechanics   but
baby did we click   and
was I lovesick stuck
on you.

At twenty you were explosive,
I an old flame
creeping close again.
I poured cold water on the science   but
boy o boy we flashed we fused we flared
spearing the dark night air
with our illuminating love affair.

At thirty you were positive
I was negative.
I day you night
we chased each other's light
round the world   round the clock   round the bend
never quite apart but never could we spend
time to talk, to think, to get it right.

(But on magic days Mother Moon and Father Sun
would mount the sky together, hang around a while
reflect each other's rays of love
make the children point and smile.)

We were positive we were negative yet
with our little additions
and despite our short divisions
I reckon we added up
to a pretty neat equation.

At fifty we sit static on a shelf
dusty bookends leaning lazily against
the lifetime's words we've propped between us.

The science of it now seems simple.
The essence of sweet love boils down
to sitting tight and
finding perfect balance.

The Creation of Eve

PAULA JENNINGS

Adam in the garden,
bored with games God always wins,
the sacred logic thrusting harder,
deflating Adam's intellectual ardour.

Adam, chafed and sullen,
beginning to finger sharp stones
and big sticks;
beginning not to hide the discontented glare
beneath that blond, divinely-crafted hair.

God is no fool.
Unkillable, but shy of violent scenes,
he wishes not to rock the cosmic boat
by having Adam try to cut his throat.

God moves fast;
stuffs Adam with a spirit,
lets him strut and swell
then plucks from him a sort of manikin
whose holy task will be to let his Adam win.

A Poem About Smiling at Women in the Street

PAULA JENNINGS

Jennifer smiles at women in the street,
lapping them with a warm 'we are',
gathering a prickly-glittery fine bouquet
of wry grin 'it's a dog's life for a woman',
of cold glare 'don't look at me, dyke',
of blank stare 'who's she smiling at?'
of wide smile 'yes sister — us',

Jennifer smiles and stomps the pavement,
blistering concrete with her courage,
warming roots that will leaf our new world.

Venus

PAULA JENNINGS

You drifted languidly to shore;
perched on a shell;
one hand modest on your crotch.
the other ineffectual on your breast.
You looked dazed
and you were worrying about your hair.

If only you had surfed in,
the ocean gripped between your thighs,
or walked the water, braiding clouds and waves,
translating power into grace —

If you had taught us that wild balance
we could have named you love.

Magician

PAULA JENNINGS

I have invented you,
distilled you from scattered longings
(alchemist narcissus),
conjured you from grief;
from your loving tiger eyes this monstrous gold,
our blurred boundaries roaring with discovery.
Kindred, you said,
kindred spirit,
handing me the crucible.

And now,
when you say we are separate,
I can only smile.

Better Than Beer And Skittles

Lynne Bryan

FRANK DROPS me off outside the sisters' flat. He waves goodbye in that leather-clad way of his before accelerating down the road. I watch a while, seeing how his bike's suspension copes with the potholes and uneven tarmac. Then I remove my helmet and shake my hair, which is a silly move because I've very little hair to shake. I had it cut a couple of days ago by my brother's girlfriend, Geena. She smokes as she cuts and I half expected to have the singed look, but she's done a good job. She's clipped it up the back, but kept the fringe long. This is fine by me. I have this habit of pushing my fringe off my face when I talk, so I would miss it if it got the chop. Frank says, 'You doing that so I can read your lips?' I don't take offence. The sisters confide that before I visit they always turn their hearing aids up a notch — 'to catch your dulcet tones'.

Frank and I are going through a rough patch. It's all to do with my visits here: every Tuesday night I come, regular as clockwork, and at first he accepted it. But now the work's beer and skittles has been moved to a Tuesday, and he's pissed off that I'd sooner be with the sisters than with workmates. I tell him the sisters' is like a breath of fresh air; that I don't want to spend my evenings with the same people I stand next to during the day. It's hard enough as it is to last my forty-hour week cooped up with Marjorie and Sheila and the rest packing those sausage rolls, six rolls to a box, every roll three inch by one inch, every box red- and orange-striped 'Authentic English Pork'. I dream of sausage rolls. I dream that Marjorie and Sheila and the rest push the rolls one after the other down my throat until I gag and balloon and finally burst — my insides, my brain, my heart, nothing but sausage roll. Frank says I'm too sensitive and swears he'll run off with Louise, the mini-skirted dwarf from Quality Control. But I know he won't. We have something, Frank and I. When we get together, it's fireworks. Yes.

'Hello, love,' says Helen, tapping me on the shoulder as I stroll up the entry.

'Hiya,' I say. 'Is he out there again tonight?'

'I'm afraid so,' says Helen. 'I've pleaded with him, but he says he's doing no harm; just checking his wife's up to nothing immoral.'

'Immoral,' I say. 'Big word.' I look past Helen's shoulder and can just make out the front end of a blue Cortina. Inside, I know, sits her husband, Derek, a fat man with no taste. He wears bright orange and red lumberjack shirts, shiny tracksuit bottoms, and shoes with Cuban heels. He's about fifty and believes the sisters' is a knocking shop. Ever since Helen's first visit six months ago he's parked his car, and fingers drumming against the dashboard, has waited to catch her at it. A diseased mind. He must know by now that only women visit the sisters'. Perhaps he thinks we're porno dykes and our sewing-boxes hide kinky sex aids: strap-on willies, massage oils, a whip, a chain, a crutchless panty, and a peek-a-boo bra. I doubt though that he'd be able to think of such things. He's the type of man whose mind can only cope with the missionary position; the dainty woman lying back and thinking of England, the bulldog pumping her from above. Do I sound bitter? Mmm, perhaps I had too many of those nights myself, before I met Frank and his amazing bag of tricks.

'Rose phoned the other day,' says Helen, slipping the key into the sisters' front-door lock. 'Asked me to bring some Fisherman's Friends. Apparently Ivy has a summer cold. She's been in bed on and off the past week.'

'Got to be careful at her age,' I say, pushing open the door.

We step into the flat. I love this flat. The sisters haven't changed a thing for years. The wallpaper is old, creamy, and covered in pink roses. The carpets are worn thin and have lost a lot of their colour. Everywhere smells fusty, like the insides of my nephew's duffel bag; the one he uses for P.E.

Rose has come out of the Quilting Room to greet us. 'Did you manage to get the Fisherman's Friends?' she asks. Helen nods and fumbles in her dress pocket for them.

'For fuck's sake,' shouts Jean, her voice husky from fags, reaching us from the room. 'Grab her before she collapses. Eighty-eight is not the age to go chasing Fisherman's Friends.'

'I've always liked a sailor,' jokes Rose. She's wearing her green dress again, which suits her. It is very low at the front and reveals her thin breasts. Sue always dangles a necklace between her breasts. Today it's her fruit and nut necklace, made from varnished hazelnuts and wood cut to look like a slice of pear or peach or apple. She must have been a real goer when young. Don't know why she never married, probably had more sense.

I follow Rose and Helen into the Quilting Room. Jean gives us a queenly wave of welcome, whilst Ivy smiles. Two years older than Rose, Ivy looks like she's at death's door. Her hair is very white, though she wears it down in a girlie way, with clips holding it from her eyes. Jean bought her the clips for her last birthday. One is a luminous orange that glows in the dark, the other is pink with gold glitter sprinkled on it. She also has a lime-green headband which is dotted with huge cream daisies, but she only wears this when she feels like partying. The horrible thing about Ivy is her skin. It is very wrinkled and covered in large brown blotches. It hangs off her like she's lost a lot of weight. Poor Ivy. She looks flushed. It must be her cold, or perhaps it's the sunlight shining through the window. It glows around her head like a halo.

'Come and sit down,' says Jean, sewing to the left of Ivy. Jean is the one who got me into this. She's a funny woman: funny ha ha and funny peculiar. She gets obsessions.

She was first married to Lyle, still alive, a good-looking bloke who runs the local pop round. Jean talks of him fondly. 'The first you marry for love, the second for money,' she says. Lyle was a real love. When Jean gets on the vodkas and limes she tells of how Lyle made her heart beat. She remembers hot, exciting nights. Lyle is no missionary position man. He's inventive. But Jean is into status. She couldn't live for long with a man whose sole income comes from selling lemonade. So she ran off with George. George is the opposite of Lyle. He's short for a start, but he's also rich. He owns a chain of discount stores; those shops where you can get sanitary towels made from shredded cardboard for 20p a dozen. The type of shop that is doing our Ozone. His hairsprays are lethal. Geena uses them on the blue rinse OAPs, those that like their hair to be stiff as a corpse. She warns them though not to stand too close to a fire or to her fag or else they'll end up the corpse. But George is not all bad. He bought Jean her patchwork and quilting shop; something she'd been hankering after for ages. She loves her business. She claims that patchwork is an important art form, that it speaks volumes about women. She goes on about this, strutting around her shop like the original burn your bra. Silly cow. I say to Jean that she's not liberated, that she's owned by George. But she won't have it. 'I chose him,' she says. 'I'm in control.' And that was how I first met her, doing her I'm in control bit, when I went to Mother Goose to buy some cottons. She seized me by the shoulders and pointed out a notice.

'*Help!*' it said, in a scrawly spider hand. '*We are two ancient ladies trying to achieve the impossible. Fifteen years ago we set ourselves the task of sewing quilts for all our nephews and nieces. We have managed to sew a quilt a year so far, but we still have four quilts to go. As our eyesight and everything else is failing we would appreciate a hand with these remaining quilts. Once a week will do. Tuesdays at 7.00 p.m. Come to Lower Flat, 20 Kennedar Drive. Tea and biscuits served. Mind next-door's Alsatian.*'

'I think,' said Jean, 'that we ought to attend this, you and I. I can see you're the type who's looking for something extra. Be a change, get you away from chasing the men, hey?'

Frank told me to steer clear, but there's something about Jean that's very persuasive. She has this face that dares you. She's pulling it now, because I'm refusing to settle. It takes me a while to start my sewing. I like to wander, to look at my friends, to chat. I'm like a bee droning about every place but on the flower where I should be, sucking up my honey.

'Samantha, you got ants in your pants?' says Jean.

'She's just admiring the decor,' smiles Ivy, who knows the way I go about things.

'It's nice,' I say. 'I know what to expect when I come here.'

'A tip,' chuckles Rose, passing the packet of Fisherman's Friends to her elder sister. Ivy opens the packet. She pulls out a sweet and drops it into her skinny mouth.

'Yuk,' she says.

When Jean and I first turned up at the sisters' we had a bit of a shock. They are not your normal, everyday old ladies; not at all like Granny, stuck as she is in the past with nothing in her head but death. No, Rose and Ivy have spunk, ambition. They began their quilting marathon when Rose turned seventy, Ivy seventy-two. They pooled their savings to buy a huge quilting frame, which they assembled from kit form in their living-room, now called the Quilting Room. In their hurry, they didn't clear the room to make a real space for the frame, but they pushed every piece of furniture outwards. Even now their sofa, telly, radio, book-case, drinks bar, and aquarium line the walls of the room like they are second-hand goods waiting for the rag and bone man. The aquarium is best.

It stands on the sofa and the fish swim back and forth against a backdrop of cream and brown stripes. Jean, when she first saw this, thought of contacting the sea-creatures branch of the RSPCA, but changed her mind. The fish look healthy. There are always six of them and they always shine golden, not white like they are sickening. OAP fishes. Per-haps they live off the dust that hangs like curtains in this topsy-turvey room. 'The Twilight Zone,' says Frank, when I talk about it. 'Strange things happen to those who enter the Twilight Zone. Little old ladies turn into willy weirdo witches. Watch out. They'll strap you to their frame one of these days, and will suck you of your youth and beauty.' Beauty! I often tell Frank that he should write, such a vivid imagination he's got. But he says he has no time, that he's devoted to becoming a world-class beer and skittles man. Could be Jean's right: 'The first you marry for love, the second for money.'

Today, Jean is dressed in her Spanish costa packet outfit. A bolero trouser suit made out of red felt-like fabric and fringed with black tassels. She looks a bugger, but somehow carries it off. Confidence, I suppose. Helen, who has taken my place beside Jean, is a different kind of woman. She's into British Home Stores Specials. Make her look kind of dowdy, but no doubt her husband wouldn't want her to dress in anything more appealing.

Helen joins us ladies off her own bat. She heard about Ivy and Rose through the neighbourhood grapevine. She loves sewing, wanted to be a needlework teacher once, and so defied her husband for the very first time and came here. She reminds Ivy of her and Rose's mother: a small sweet person who was married to a drayman. His first love was beer, the second horses. Women weren't noticed until they didn't get dinner on time. Same with Helen's husband. He didn't take much notice of her until she started trekking out on Tuesday nights. Then he started playing the grand old man Possessive. Sometimes Helen mentions how she makes him a treat steak-and-kidney to butter him up, mostly though she keeps her mouth shut. She pushes him to one side like he's a nasty mess that needs seeing to, but not before she has had her fun. Her sewing box is neat and tidy, a real tool of pleasure. The quilting cottons are arranged in colour order; the needles stuck in straight lines in the padded lid of the box; her thimble, which she slips onto her finger now, having a special resting place wrapped in a lace hanky. 'Touch the quilt, Samantha,' says Helen to me, looking at it like a lover.

'Beautiful,' I say, running my hand, which I've checked to see is clean, over the ivory and cream silk and the teeny-weeny quilting stitches. The quilt is the sisters' last, their nineteenth. It's for their great-great-great-niece who is ten years old. All the quilts that the sisters have sewn take away the breath, but this one can't be beat.

Ivy and Rose have quilted from the year dot. They made quilts for their mother from scraps. The quilts were usually used for bedding, though Ivy has told us how her mother once persuaded their landlord to take a crazy quilt in exchange for a fortnight's free rent. Jean thinks this is a wonderful story and has added it to her patchwork museum that she's set up above her shop. She got Ivy to write it out, and has stuck it with a picture of a crazy quilt on a display board under the heading 'Quilts *vs* homelessness. Women do it again!' A lovely image I say, but I bet many landlords, even in the old days, would sooner have had a bit of the other. I know my landlord, when I'm behind with the readies, wants payment with some up and under. But I'm not having it: once they're in your pants, they're hard to get out. Got to be careful in this twentieth century. One man, a heavy-duty rubber, and a closed back passage. Simple pleasures.

'This seat taken?' I ask Rose, plonking myself down on the only free chair in the room. A wonky chair, it rocks in time to your sewing arm.

'It's yours, no strings,' says Rose, smiling.

'Why thanks.' I rest my sewing box on my knee. I click it open, and rummage through my jumble of cottons and pins and needles and templates. 'Do you think this is going to wash alright?' I mutter for the sake of muttering.

'The quilt?' asks Helen.

'Mmm.' I find a decent needle and thread it through my jumper so I can't lose it.

'Don't see why not,' says Jean.

'Well those dresses were never meant for washing. You're only supposed to wear them once.'

'Nothing to worry about, I washed them when we got them home, and they were okay,' says Ivy, looking as if she couldn't wash a pair of pants, let alone four wedding dresses. 'We always do this for every quilt. You should know, Samantha.'

'Sorry, I forgot,' I say, remembering quick, for the sisters still use what they learnt when small. For a start they never buy new fabrics. They use old fabrics, liked used clothes or curtains. They wash them, then play around with them, matching this and that, before cutting them up and sewing them into quilts. Making something new and different from something else. The sisters say that by reusing fabrics they add a little extra to the quilts. (I agree. I watched a programme once where this woman, whose daughter had died, made a quilt out of the daughter's summer dresses, so that when she slept beneath the quilt she felt her daughter was still alive in some way, close to her. 'Spooky,' said Frank, bullied into watching. 'Too arty-farty for her own good.' But Frank has no idea: he can't get his head round this nineteenth quilt at all, made as it is from wedding dresses.)

Jean helped the sisters get the dresses. She took them out to Bridal Delight, which is on the verge of bankruptcy — too many youngsters living in the big S for Sin — and they bought them at the cheapest of prices. The sisters wanted wedding dresses because they want this quilt to say something about being pure. I say a wedding dress in this modern world is more than a sure sign that the bride's been tried and tested. Second-hand goods, but clean second-hand goods — if you get my drift — is all that's wanted now. A disease-free bride. But Rose and Ivy won't have it. They believe their dresses speak of innocent things like the Virgin Mary; like their old age without sex; like their little niece who is still before sex. Frank tells me that this last part is crap, loads of his friends reckon they know ten year-olds who are dying for it. I say it's wishful thinking. Men like to believe there are nympho ten year-olds walking the streets, when really little girls have nothing more on their minds than hamburgers and soap stars. Perhaps when they reach twelve it's different. Twelve is when your breasts begin to show. Twelve is when John across the road touched me up in his den. My first.

I take my quilting needle from my jumper. I hold it high

so the summer sunlight shines through the eye, making it easier for me to know exactly where to stick my cotton, and I thread it. The funny thing about John is he's only supposed to have one ball, that's what Louise, the mini-skirted dwarf from Quality Control tells me, but I can't remember.

'Day-dreamer, wake up!' says Jean. She gives me a look with her hard face, before bending over the quilt again, her black back-combed hair making an ugly spider shadow upon the silk. Perhaps I ought to introduce her to Geena and her magic scissors, but then Jean's hair is like Buckingham Palace, a national monument. It would go against God, England, and Margaret Thatcher to touch it.

I sew a stitch. 'Are you watching, Jean?' I ask.

'And about time too,' she smiles, not one to hold a grudge for long. 'We've got a lot to do on this.'

Too true. The quilt is just a plain strip quilt which suits the silk, but it's covered in real difficult stitching. Ivy and Rose don't go in for this usually: they tend to go for a tidy running stitch which follows the outline of the patchwork shapes such as SHOO-FLY or THE GRANDMOTHER'S FAN. But for this quilt they have pricked out a design of CABLE and FEATHER WREATH. It's not quite like embroidering the whole quilt, but it's close. Time consuming. We've been at it for nine months. The sisters joke they've made this last piece so fiddly to delay things. They're afraid, as we all are, about what's going to happen once this last quilt is sewn.

Jean has pressed the sisters to hold an exhibition of all nineteen quilts, once the nineteenth is finished, in her museum. A good idea for her business, certainly draw in the crowds, but, as she admitted to Helen on the quiet, it would give the sisters something to look forward to. The sisters said no. They're unsure if all the nephews and nieces have kept their quilts, whether all would be returned, whether they'd look as clean and good as when they were made.

They told Jean that they'd be upset to see tea stains or egg stains or sick or sex upon their handiwork. So they turned down the offer, as usual not mincing their words.

'You're beginning to fill out, Samantha,' says Rose, stitching expert and fast, proving my point.

'Tell me about it,' I mutter. Frank has been saying the same thing. Says my breasts are getting heavier and my belly more rounded. He wants a kid so he's hoping that's the reason. I'm hoping it's age creeping on. Once you hit twenty-five they do say that the body goes. I don't want my body to go, but I'd sooner that than a kiddy. I can't face the thought of squeezing one out: the pain. I don't like pain. And what happens when it gets to be a teenager? Teenagers treat mothers like shit. I threw a can of tomato soup at my mother when she wouldn't allow me at fifteen to go to the Free and Easy Singles Disco down Canal Street. It hit her on the thigh: I was aiming for her heart.

'Oh, but I think it suits you,' says Ivy. 'Bonny. You can be too thin, you know.' She snuffles and rummages in her pocket for a Fisherman's Friend.

'Thinness equals meanness of spirit. Look at me!' laughs Rose.

'Your spirit is far from mean,' says Helen quietly.

But I can't be bothered with this, I'm rattled. 'Well, I'm not pregnant if that's what you're getting at,' I nip. 'Precaution is the name of the game with me.' I stitch the curve of a Cable badly, and tutting begin to unpick the thread.

'There's nothing wrong with being pregnant,' says Jean. She's speaking with her head bent more so over the quilt. 'I loved it.'

'You pregnant!' What a revelation. I thought Jean was the original Mrs Contraception. I stop my sewing.

'Mmm,' says Jean. 'Didn't last long. Lyle got me humping round his crates of pop. I lost it. Just sat down on the toilet and there it went. Whoosh. Like a big period.'

'But that's awful,' I say. Jean has never opened up like this before. Usually she is jokey or all strident new woman. Perhaps I should hug her or something, but she doesn't look huggable in that bull-fighter's outfit. I can see Helen and Rose and Ivy are thinking the same. So awkward. Ivy is losing herself in her hanky, whilst Rose touches her necklace like she has prayer beads in her hands. Helen just looks shocked, doubly-shocked, because suddenly there he is pressing his outsized nose against the window pane.

'I know you're in there,' shouts Helen's husband. 'I know what you're doing. You bitch. Has he got it up you yet? You're breaking my heart.' He raises a hand to shade his eyes, trying to see into the room.

Jean is first off the mark. She helps Ivy from her chair. 'Better move back, just in case,' she says.

'Yes,' I whisper, watching the orange and red lumberjack shirt as it sways backwards, forwards. It blocks out the usual view of the sisters' flower boxes, stray dogs, kids and council flats. I begin to wish next-door's Alsatian, which used to cause us so much trouble, hadn't died. It would've sunk its teeth into Derek for sure.

'Getting enough are you? Enjoying yourself?' the bully shouts. 'I can see you. I can see you.' He bangs his fists hard against the glass. Thump. Thump. Thump. Thump. Bloody big fists, like flesh-covered boxing gloves. I wonder whether he uses them on Helen: she's never actually said.

'I'll go out to him,' she murmurs. She looks afraid, shrunk into her flowery dress.

'No don't,' says Rose, 'that's what he's wanting.'

'Too right,' says Jean, stepping up to the window.

'For fuck's sake,' I say, pushing my fringe off my face. Old habits die hard even in troubled times. 'What are you playing at?'

Jean flaps a hand. 'I'm going to teach this bastard a lesson.'

She pulls back her bolero jacket to undo the blouse beneath. One by one the buttons slip from their holes. Easy. 'George likes this outfit,' she smiles. 'It's husband friendly.'

Ivy, Rose, Helen and me: we are quiet. Can't say a word. There is Jean and she looks magnificent. The blouse has fallen open and there shines her body — brown, healthy and perfect. Her breasts are much better than mine. They are big, motherly, but they don't sag. They are powerful. A black tassel fringing her bolero rests just above the left nipple; it's a finishing touch. She looks like a painting hung on the wrong wall, because all the while, behind her, stands this pathetic angry man.

Jean turns to face him. 'Watch my technique, girls,' she says. She begins to rub herself against the pane, up and down, up and down. I can only see her back, but it's enough for me. I squeal, excited: my head full of lovely tits pressing fat and warm upon the icy glass.

'Ooohh,' I squeal. 'Ooohh.'

'Schh, Samantha, schh,' whispers Helen, her eyes brighter, no longer frightened. 'You'll spoil her concentration.'

'You know,' says Rose, huddling up, 'that kind of wriggle takes years of practice. I myself have never mastered the art.'

'Monroe,' says Ivy, 'she had it.'

'Oh quiet,' says Helen. 'Jean's having problems, can't you see? I reckon Derek needs glasses.'

And true, it looks like Jean's show is wasted. Helen's husband peers through the window, blind as a bat to her gorgeous flesh. Till she stretches up, pretending to kiss him. Then it registers, and it's like he's witnessed death. His face turns a ghastly white, and he begins to back from the window, his arms held out, sweat patches darkening his lumberjack shirt. 'That's it, boy?' shouts Jean, triumphant. 'You've no idea, have you?' She works her body wilder now, like an upmarket belly dancer.

'Never,' says Ivy, 'have I seen anything so... '

'Marvellous,' laughs Rose. 'And look at Derek. What a Derek! He's been hit between the eyes!'

'Enough,' shouts Jean. She spins round and with a final nifty move draws the Quilting Room curtains on the man.

'Wonderful,' I say. 'Bloody wonderful.' I imagine Derek stumbling to his Cortina, see him tripping over his own feet — so confused is he, so winded.

I reach for the lamp, which stands on top of the sisters' drinks bar, and I switch it on. The lamp has an orange glass shade and the light that shines through it makes the room glow magical. The quilt shimmers. The water in the aquarium appears a dark blue like the deepest blue of the sea where Whales and Sting Rays swim. I feel very safe, and I can see that Helen and Rose and Ivy and Jean, who has buttoned her blouse, feel very safe too. There's a Famous Five feeling. Yes.

'I believe there are a few old bottles of rum and gin and perhaps sherry in that bar,' says Rose.

'And glasses,' adds Ivy. 'Nice ones too. If I remember rightly they have a pattern of gold crisscrosses around the brims.'

'I could do with a drink,' admits Helen. 'Make mine a large one.'

I sit with Rose and Ivy and Helen and Jean around the quilting frame. We slug our glasses of booze, making sure not a drop spills upon the quilt, but going for it all the same. 'You know,' I say, 'Frank's been trying to get me to jack this in. Wants me to go to the work's beer and skittles night instead.'

'But this is much better than beer and skittles,' says Ivy,

poking around in her Fisherman's Friends packet for another sweet.

'I know,' I smile. 'And what's more I don't think you should be mixing cough stuff with the strong stuff.'

'You tell her,' laughs Jean, trying to run her hand through her black back-combed hair, but getting her fingers stuck halfway.

Only a Mouse

For Peter Attle

VALERIE THORNTON

And he's left me
only a mouse;
a little piece of curved lead
crimped around a long, long tail
of dirty string
which linked us, laughing,
him above and me below,
easing a new cord
through my bedroom window frame.

I carry it with me
now that he has gone,
curled against my heart
as I hold this forlorn cord,
me above and him below,
easing him into the ground
quieter than any mouse
within his leaded box.

The Contributors

ALISON ARMSTRONG was born in 1964 and is a Sassenach living in Alloa. 'The Cockney Piper' was partly based on experiences as a probationary schoolteacher. Subsequent work in Adult Education has led her to believe that the story was prophetic.

LYNNE BRYAN was born in England in 1961. She moved to Glasgow four years ago after completing the MA in Creative Writing at the University of East Anglia. Currently working for a Women's Support Project, she writes in her spare time. 'Better Than Beer and Skittles' is her first published piece.

ALISON CAMPBELL is from Aberdeen and presently lives in North London, where she is completing counselling training. Co-editor of *The Man Who Loved Presents* (The Women's Press, 1991), an anthology of seasonal stories by women.

SUSAN CHANEY was born in Cambridge in 1951 and brought up in Cornwall. She has lived in Edinburgh for the past nineteen years and has three children. Apart from writing she works part-time as an Adult Education Tutor with women's groups. Has had several short stories published and is now working on a novel.

MAGGIE CHRISTIE lives in Edinburgh and makes her living copy-editing, indexing and proofreading. Her poems have appeared in *Fresh Oceans* (Stramullion) and *Whatever You Desire* (Oscars). She has won a prize in the Edinburgh Writers' Association poetry performance competition. Radical feminist, a born-again oboeist and a member of Pomegranate Women's Writing Group.

BARBARA CLARKE lives and works in Edinburgh and has aspirations to do the same in the Americas. She has published work in various magazines and anthologies.

MARGARET ELPHINSTONE has worked as a gardener and a writer, and has recently published gardening books, as well as two novels and, most recently, a collection of short stories, *An Apple From a Tree* (Women's Press, 1991). She is currently working on her third novel and teaches English Studies at the University of Strathclyde. She has two daughters.

FRANZESKA G. EWART chose a career in Primary education after graduating in zoology and now teaches in a small, multicultural school in Glasgow. Enjoys the opportunities this gives to share love of writing, art and in particular puppetry. Likes to escape to the country whenever possible. First published work for adults.

JANICE GALLOWAY was born in Ayrshire and now lives in Glasgow. Her first novel, *The Trick is To Keep Breathing* (Polygon, 1990) was shortlisted for the Whitbread prize first novel category. More recently, she has had a collection of short stories published, *Blood* (Secker and Warburg, 1991).

MAGI GIBSON was born in 1953 in Gargunnock, near Stirling. Her poems have been published in *Cencrastus*, *The Scotsman*, *Chapman*, and in the anthologies *Fresh Oceans* (Stramullion), *Meantime* (Polygon) and *I Wouldn't Thank You for a Valentine* (Viking). 1989 Prize winner in Women 2000 / *Scotland on Sunday* Competition and Edinburgh Writers' Association Poetry Performance Competition.

PAULA JENNINGS was born in Fife and celebrates lesbian feminism in her writing and in other political / spiritual adventures. Her poetry has been published in *One Foot on the Mountain*, *Spinster* and *Fresh Oceans*. Has contributed to feminist debate in a number of books and periodicals.

ALISON KENNEDY was born in Dundee and lives in Glasgow. She holds an SAC residency in Hamilton and East Kilbride and co-ordinates creative writing for Project Ability. Her first collection of short stories, *Night Geometry and the Garscadden Trains* won the Saltire / *Scotsman* First Book of the Year award for 1991. She is currently completing a novel.

ALISON KERMACK lives in Edinburgh. Her first poetry collection has been published by Clocktower Press, South Queensferry, in 1991.

HELEN LAMB is a graduate of Glasgow University and now lives in Dunblane with her three children. Her work has previously appeared in *Original Prints* Two, *Fresh Oceans*, *Scottish Child* and has been broadcast on Radio Four's Morning Story.

V.J. MCCALL lives in Edinburgh with her two daughters. She has previously been published in *Scottish Child*. Her poem, 'Some Days', is written in memory of her sister Eileen who died of cancer in 1986.

ANNE MACLEOD was born in the Highlands of Anglo-Irish parents. She studied medicine at the University of Aberdeen but has lived and worked in Inverness ever since. Has had work published in various places, notably *Lines Review*, *Cencrastus*, *Aberdeen University Review* and *Meantime*.

OLIVIA MACMAHON is of Irish origin but has lived in Aberdeen for over twenty years and has two grown-up Scottish children. She has worked as a teacher and teacher trainer of English as a Foreign Language in many countries including Poland, France and Egypt.

CATHERINE MACPHAIL was born in Greenock. She has had short stories and humorous articles published as well as two romantic novels. Has also ghosted a work of non-fiction. Her first love however is humour, especially Scottish humour — latest venture is a situation comedy.

LINDA MCCANN has taught Creative Writing at Glasgow University's Adult Education Department. She has had poetry and short stories published and is currently working on a collection of each.

MARY MCCANN was born in Ayrshire, studied in Glasgow and lives in Edinburgh. She started writing and drawing while unemployed. Member of Pomegranate. Enjoys taking part in readings. Has written a play *Thunderbirds and Snakebites* for Catch Theatre Co.; interviewed in *Sleeping with Monsters* (Polygon, 1989).

LINDSAY MCKRELL lives in Stirling but works in Airdrie as a community librarian. She has had poetry published in *Original Prints* Two and Three, *Poetry North* and *Poetry Now* and a short play, *Small Change*, commissioned and performed in Stirling. She has been in semi-retirement due to excessive study but is beginning to write again.

ANGELA MCSEVENEY was born in 1964 and lives in Edinburgh. She has published poems in previous volumes of *Original Prints*. She presently works as a library assistant. Her first collection of poetry will be published by Polygon in Autumn 1992.

JANET PAISLEY was born in London, brought up in Avonbridge and now lives in Glen Village, near Falkirk. She has published many short stories in English and Scots appearing in, among others, *The New Makars*, *Original Prints*, *Gown*, *Interarts*, *Lines Review* and *Scottish Child*. Currently, Janet is Writing Fellow, Glasgow District Libraries, South division.

HONOR PATCHING lives in Fife. This is her first venture into print. She was born in Scotland and is just beginning to write full-time.

SYLVIA PEARSON, born in Edinburgh, has been 'writing in her head' for most of her life. Having run out of space, she has decided to put her work on paper. Currently compiling a collection of South African short stories.

CHRISTINE QUARRELL was born in Glasgow, still lives and works there. She has two sons aged twenty-three and fourteen. 'Through poetry comes a letting-go and healing of pain.'

ALISON REID was born in 1957 and currently lives in East Kilbride. Works and performs with a writer's group, Bread and Circuses, she has had material published in *Radical Scotland* and *West Coast Magazine*.

JENNY ROBERTSON lives in Edinburgh and has had a poetry collection published by Chapman. She also teaches creative writing at Queen Margaret College.

MAUREEN SANGSTER was born in Aberdeen and now lives in Kirkcaldy where she teaches creative writing to adults. Her poetry has been published in various magazines and anthologies including *Chapman*, *West Coast Magazine*, *Different People* (Straightline Publications) and *Fresh Oceans* (Stramullion).

VALERIE THORNTON was born in 1954 in Glasgow. Educated in Stirling and at Glasgow University. Gave up teaching English five years ago and has had a variety of odd jobs since including work on feature films, film festivals, picture research and writing advertising copy.

Currently subtitling for the BBC and teaching creative writing. Work published in various literary magazines and anthologies over the past eight years.

JANETTE WALKINSHAW, who has had stories in *Original Prints* One and Two, now lives in Ayrshire. Her work as a solicitor leaves her little time for writing but she is presently working on a stage play.

DOREEN WATSON is an early-retired Senior Health Education Officer with Greater Glasgow Health Board, writing since 1989 with a local group.

FIONA WILSON was brought up in Aberdeen and studied literature at Glasgow University. Since 1988, she has lived in New York where she works in publishing and is completing a post-graduate degree in the Creative Writing Program at New York University. She will be teaching Poetry workshop in the coming year. Her work has previously appeared in American publications including *Amelia* and *Ark*.

Other books published by Polygon

Night Geometry and the Garscadden Trains

A.L. Kennedy

£7.95 paperback

Winner of the Saltire Society/*Scotsman* First Book of the Year
Award for 1991.

A.L. Kennedy's first collection of short stories shows a talented individual at work.

Her characters are often alone and sometimes lonely as they ponder the mysteries of sex, death and public transport at the end of the twentieth century. Written with empathy and wit, her intimate narratives expose vast areas of feeling beneath the surface of ordinary lives. Often focused on single women, these stories give voice to individuals who are neither happy in their singularity nor content within relationships.

...an eclectic collection mostly written when she was only in her very early twenties - she speaks with a voice of almost unnerving maturity.'
The Scotsman

Kennedy is a compassionate writer, who strives to feel her way within her characters and allow them to speak their lives.'
Times Literary Supplement

A Sparrow's Flight

Margaret Elphinstone

£8.95 paperback

In a kind of future which bears a strong relation to the past, two travellers, Naomi and Thomas, embark on a month-long journey which parallels the inner journey that each also has to make. Their experiences are mirrored in the imagery of the Tarot, and in the folk tradition of the country in which they find themselves. The journey itself forms a spiral: it takes the characters into the heart of a wasteland which is a combination of actual place, literary mythology, and the realisation of our contemporary fears. Then it leads them on to the point where they started - the passing month has altered the tides and the weather, and neither Naomi nor Thomas returns to the exact place they left. Their journey is set in the Borders, and during the course of it they unknowingly cross and re-cross a border which does not exist for them, but for us remains an ambiguous image of shifting reality.

'It is a most pleasant respite from this world to live through *A Sparrow's Flight* with such a fine writer in charge of our destiny.'

Chapman

'..it's intensely human, about how a small group of people relate, about how women find new roles and problems in a new society, and about sexual redefinition.'

Books in Scotland

Ophelia
and other poems

Elizabeth Burns

£6.95 paperback

Elizabeth Burns is a new voice in poetry: her meditative, tender tones sometimes exchanged for an incensed reminder of those who cannot make themselves heard. She has a painter's patience with texture, light, landscapes, and a sensuous appreciation of taste and scent. Her histories are those coded in women's embroideries, in Ophelia's laments, in the fortunes of a Southern portrait, in the sleevenotes of a MacDiarmid reader: she dwells on the intimacies of love and friendship. The delicacy of her attention is matched by the rhythms and spaces of her verse.

...her fluid forms and sensuous images have an almost mesmerising effect.'

The Herald

Brimming with the imagery of rich, ripe fruit, flowers; rejoicing in the fecundity of nature, human intimacy, heady scents, the rhythms of the sea and love, they remain perceptive and unsentimental due to the great delicacy of her touch.'

Scotland on Sunday

Her imagination can touch ours - and surely this, if anything, is a proof of poetry.'

The Scotsman

All Polygon books are available from your nearest bookshop
or can be ordered direct from the publisher.

Specify the titles you require and fill in the form below.

Send to: Polygon, 22 George Square, Edinburgh, EH8 9LF
                  Tel: 031 650 4689, Fax: 031 662 0053

I enclose a cheque made payable to Polygon for £............

Please debit my VISA/Mastercard

(p&p is included for UK orders, please add &1.80 per book for
overseas orders.)

NAME..

ADDRESS*..

....

....

POSTCODE......................................

CARD EXPIRY DATE..................................
*Supply both delivery & cardholder's address if different.

☐   Tick here for a copy of our recent catalogue